UGLY MONEY

Writer Will Adams' young niece, Marisa, has learned from her parents, film director Jack Adams and his wife Ruth, that Jack is not her real father. Reluctantly, Will agrees to help Marisa to find the man who is. But a shock awaits him: it looks as if Marisa's biological father is Scott Hartman, a fabulously wealthy recluse. A bitter man, Hartman makes a decision concerning Marisa's future that is to unleash a wave of violence, threatening to engulf not just Marisa, but her entire family.

1

Marisa

1

I HEARD the other day about a man who was having breakfast, reading the paper and minding his own business, when a bulldozer came crashing through the wall of his house. Imagine it: as the plaster dust clears, there you are looking at this gigantic piece of machinery where your nice new kitchen used to be. Presently the driver will explain that he put the thing into Reverse when he meant Drive. It's known as Chance.

Chance pitched me headlong into this story. In my case the bulldozer was my seventeen-year-old niece, Marisa, but that makes no difference at all; an attractive and determined teenage girl can cause as much damage as any mere bulldozer. I had just reached chapter nine, which means the book was half written, and research had taken a whole year. I'm a writer, yes. My name is Will Adams, though I don't always write under it. I'm forty-three years old. I have survived marriage and the growing up of a son and daughter; I've survived divorce, which is only painful when enmity is involved — my ex-wife and I are the best of friends as long as we're not cohabiting — and, in the past week, I've also survived death by murder.

I am . . . I was, until the arrival of my niece, writing a novel set in and around the small town of Astoria, Oregon, a dozen miles from the mouth of the Columbia River, and that's why I was living there at the time in question. It's a quiet and pleasant place, its hills decorated with wonderful, sometimes comical, wooden houses built during the Victorian and Edwardian eras, and now fashionable

2

in our age of 'nostalgia': anything to escape from the mess we've made of the present day.

Astoria has never been very important, despite the wishes of successive city fathers; its wealth lay in timber and salmon, two commodities once believed to be in endless supply — we've learned otherwise. As 'the oldest settlement west of the Rockies', it was a lure for Scandinavian and Finnish fisher-folk; the wives worked in the canneries, and most of their names live on: Astorians don't rush to and fro very much. Their town has been dwindling since the 1890s, and its heyday, nothing to do with timber or salmon, was in World War Two when a naval base sent the population soaring. The marvelous beauty of its setting, wooded hills, distant mountains, mighty river, savage Pacific, has remained fairly constant in spite of creeping real estate and brutal logging: a pleasant if unexciting place to live. Into this Eden, and smack into chapter nine, came Eve with a whole basketful of serpents. It started on a stormy Monday afternoon at the beginning of September, and when we get storms up here they don't mess around: perfect weather for writing. Indeed, when the doorbell rang I had just written, 'Chapter Nine. Lewis returned to the mouth of the Columbia in November 1927. He said he was tired of traveling and had come home for a rest, but nobody in Astoria or Ilwaco believed him; they knew he'd come back because of the gold . . . '

Cursing, I abandoned my desk and opened the door on this stunning blonde with dark blue eyes. She appeared to be in her early twenties, and it took me a moment or two to realize I was looking at my brother's child Marisa, aged seventeen. I said, "Hi, Marisa, come on in." Quite a smooth reaction, all things considered, you might even say cool. If you're not cool they have this habit of walking right over your fallen body and writing you off, politely but decisively.

I'm not being wise after the event; right there and then a small stinging shock jumped from this girl to me: nervousness, even fear, sparked around her like an electrical field. She was hiding it pretty well but it was unmistakable, and it set me tingling, ready for anything. Anything? Well, that's what I thought. She had grown since I'd last seen her, hardly surprising at that age; she now had her mother's height, and with it that negligent grace tall women have to cultivate if they're not going to appear gawky. As yet she was too young to get the negligent grace quite right, so there was still a touch of gawkiness which was touching. I said, "What brings you to the Great Pacific Northwest?"

She shrugged. "I guess the Great Pacific Southwest finally got me down." Yes, she was all nervous tension, thrumming with it. I indicated the sofa, and sat in an armchair facing her. I was thinking that Labor Day had just passed; at any minute, if not right

5

now, girls of this age should be going back to school for those all-important final semesters. After Labor Day the beaches and forests fall silent again; no sound but the sigh of plastic waste, indestructible tons of it, blown by the winds of autumn.

She was looking around my apartment. "Nice."

It's the top floor of one of those Victorian houses, expertly updated and pleasantly furnished with comfortable and not incongruous things; it has a wondrous view across the Columbia to the hills of Washington State on the far side: four miles away, it's a big river. But when youngsters say 'nice' you can be pretty sure it's not just politeness; she probably meant 'big' — it does have three bedrooms. So I was ready when she added, "We stopped over in Medford last night — why can't I ever fall asleep in motels?"

Obviously this was my cue to say, "Do you want to stay here? Who's we?"

6

"He's a darling, you'll love him."

"I only have one spare bed, the other room's strictly junk."

"We can share a bed."

"Not in my house, you can't, your parents would kill me." She laughed. "Nick's gay, we often share beds."

"Where is he now?"

"Parking the car." This was some kind of evasion — it doesn't take that long to park in Astoria: an evasion and part of her nervousness.

"He's A-OK. Really. HIV negative, everything." And then, a schoolgirl: "Actually he's my best friend." There are times when you can't help loving them, even when they're conning you. And I must say it was nice just looking at her; she wore her naturally fair hair in a longish bob, so that it fell over one eye and had to be removed from time to time; I also noticed that she'd taken the trouble to use a little cologne, a little lipstick and powder, before bearding uncle in his den.

7

It seemed high time I asked after her parents.

"They're OK, I guess. He's going to direct that *Revisions* thing." She was talking about *Revisions of Life*, bestseller, bad like most of them, much admired, much touted as *the* movie of next year. I said, "Good for him. Probably get himself another Oscar."

"Rob Railton's playing the lead. They went to this dinner party and it threw them ass-wise, everybody screaming about the Railtons and their adopted baby — hear about that?"

"Kind of." Robert Railton was the current hunk actor, drooled over by women and teenagers. His wife couldn't conceive, or so they said; others were of the opinion that he couldn't sire, but you don't air that kind of opinion about the current hunk.

"Anyway," she said, "this dinner party went berserk because they'd been on some talk show, Robert and Grace, and the guy asked when were they going to tell the boy he was adopted.

8

I mean, Jeeze! He's only like eighteen months old."

"Talk-show hosts aren't paid to think."

"They both said never, and that's what started the big argument over dinner. People saying the kid had to be told some time, others saying of course not. And then a lot of crap about what age do you tell him — like sixteen with the driver's license or is that too late?" The deep blue eyes found mine. "Well, the fat was in the fire, know what I mean?"

I didn't, but kept quiet.

"They took me out next night. Vince's. It's my favorite place — they hate it, so I . . . kind of wondered." She put both elbows on her knees and both fists under her jaw, and the hair fell forward, hiding her face. "Did *you* know?"

"Did I know what?"

"He isn't my father."

"Say that again."

She sighed. "Your brother isn't my

father. They took me to Vince's to tell me. I guess they thought it would be easier than just the three of us sitting around a table at home. It's been worrying them for years." A woeful grimace. "Seventeen years, wouldn't you know."

I said, "Jesus Christ! Marisa, are you sure?"

"Sure I'm sure, they told me right there over the eggs Benedict." She jumped up from the sofa and went to the window. "Why couldn't they keep *quiet*? Why did they have to go to that stupid dinner party?"

Myself, I felt it made no difference whether she was my brother's child or not: he loved her, he'd loved her all her life. But I wasn't seventeen years old, and I wasn't the child in question. Naturally I imagined that this revelation was the cause of her desperate uneasiness. I'm afraid I was being simplistic; we were in what you might call a multi-layered situation. She said, "It's OK, I'm not going to bawl. I did all that."

"*When* did they tell you, Marisa?"

"Thursday."

Thursday, four days ago. "Have you been away from home five days?"

She was staring out at where the view would have been if it hadn't been obscured by driving rain and an early cloud-sodden twilight. She shook her head. "No. I stuck around till yesterday morning; I guess I was in shock. And Dad . . . Jack was so sweet, like he always is. He tried . . . tried to explain how they felt, but who wants explanations?" She swung around to face me again, and even if she'd already done the bawling, tears weren't far away. "Oh God, I know he loves me, I know they both do, so why the hell couldn't they both keep their mouths shut?"

I understood her anger and her emotion, but plain old adult practicality made me ask, "Marisa, do they know where you are?"

"No. And you mustn't tell them.

Don't look like that, Will — please, please don't tell them I'm here."

"They'll be worried sick."

"That makes three of us." A flash of rebellion. Obviously prevarication was called for: "OK, I won't tell them right now — which is what I ought to do."

"Not ever." She sounded like herself at eleven. It's a strange age, seventeen, balanced on the seesaw of growing up.

I said, "You know that's not fair."

"Was telling me fair?"

"I don't know. It was honest."

"Oh, honest . . . shit! Anyone can be honest, it's so damn easy, and it's a killer."

Back went the seesaw. Where did she get that kind of knowledge? Honesty a killer — and in my experience it often is.

She turned away from the window which the wind was trying to turn inside out. "When they told me . . . it was kind of weird. My mind stopped, I mean it actually wouldn't go forward and it wouldn't go back."

"Like a clogged drain."

"Exactly. And then . . . I guess somebody poured in the Drano, and I began to think again, I saw what I had to do. I must know, Will, I must find out."

That was understandable. Knowing probably wouldn't matter much in the end, could be dismissed; not knowing mattered like hell and could never be dismissed. So that was why she had appeared out of the storm on my doorstep, and in a jangling state of nerves.

"Just . . . Oh, just meet him. Once. Kind of . . . feel his genes in me, know what I mean?"

Yes. Difficult enough when you're young to discover who and what you are without a great mystery, a black hole, hanging over your head. "And you think you'll find him up here?"

"I know it. I haven't just sat around since Thursday, I've been Sherlocking."

The doorbell rang. "Nick. I'll get it." I thought she'd reacted a little too quickly, but put it down to her taut nerves; so I wasn't prepared for her to step outside and close the door on me. I could hear the murmur of voices from the hall and wondered just what they were up to.

Suddenly I was feeling very sorry for my brother Jack. Sorry for Ruth too, of course, but somehow it seemed worse for him. We're not close, we never have been: not even when we first came to the US together some twenty years ago, aged twenty-six and twenty-three respectively: the Adams brothers. It sounds like a singing duo or an ancient vaudeville act; actually we were a British director/writer team; we'd done pretty well in Europe but, like most young men, had our eyes fixed on the big time, i.e. Hollywood . . .

The front door opened again, the conference was over. Ushering him in she said, "This is Nick Deering. Nick, my . . . my not-uncle, Will Adams." And, quickly: "He says we can stay here."

14

We all grew out of the stereotyped image long ago; well, not all now I come to think of it; there are still a lot of brutish old dinosaurs clumping around. Her best, and gay, friend was a big burly boy, your Sixth Grade, high-school football boy, with a dry, strong handshake. He wasn't handsome, but there's a clean young American look which does almost as well: benign brown eyes, neatly cut brown hair falling over the wide forehead in a fringe. And when he smiled the eyes smiled too, and that's rare. But, I realized at once, he too was in a state of extreme nervous tension. Trying to rise above it he said, "Hi. Get the story?"

"Some of it."

"Ballbreaker, ain't it? You're not going to call your brother?"

"Not yet anyway." Carefully, I added, "Look, it may be none of my business, in which case you'll tell me so — but why are you both jumping like junkies in need of a fix?"

They glanced at each other. Marisa

said, "No reason really. I mean . . . it's no big deal."

Her best friend shook his head. "For Pete's sake, we need help, why mess around? And what do you mean, no big deal? Someone tried to run us off the road, could've killed us."

"He was just smashed, he was nothing to do with it."

Nick sighed. "Like I *know* I'm seventeen and you don't, that's the problem."

She gave him a sweet smile. I could see she'd been telling the exact truth — her best friend; she could certainly have done worse. "You're probably right, you usually are."

"So," I said, "is this where I ask, 'What do you mean, ran you off the road, could have killed you?' Or do I just wait?"

Nick spread large hands. "We goofed."

"No," said Marisa, "*I* goofed." And to me, "It's a long story, and it won't make sense unless you hear it from the beginning."

"Then tell it from the beginning."

"Really?"

"The night is young. When did you two last eat?"

"Around noon."

"Right. You can talk while I cook. Fettucini OK?"

"Marinara?" Sophisticated Hollywood brat!

"Sure. Clams, mussels, squid."

"Super!"

"So come in the kitchen. Fix drinks. Mine's a gin and French, and I don't mean a Martini — half gin, half Noilly Prat, on the rocks."

★ ★ ★

Why am I writing this story instead of going back to chapter nine as I ought? Because I resent people who try to kill me, and because it's there — same for writers as it is for mountaineers.

Chance, the same implacable joker that motivated the bulldozer, led me by the nose off the highway and into

17

the American wilderness. And for the benefit of my fellow-Europeans, let me add that leaving the highway in this neck of the woods doesn't mean a stroll through the bluebells; the underbrush is full of nasty surprises like poison oak and poison ivy, a person can get hurt. Semi-human creatures also dwell there; they can cause you irreparable harm and won't hesitate to do so if your interests, or those of your beautiful niece, conflict with theirs. They have no moral sense, money is their only morality, and you don't beat them because they're ten thousand times richer than you are. The law doesn't beat them because it doesn't want to — they can afford the best attorneys, and they give *so* generously to the policemen's ball and the President's ball and all the balls in between.

2

So while I cooked, my favorite pastime after writing and messing around in boats, and while Nick chopped garlic — an irritating job, it always sticks to the knife — Marisa perched herself on a stool at the counter and began to tell me from the beginning.

When her mind began to operate again after the initial shock and the anger that went with it, certainty swept over her like a cold Pacific wave, and she was amazed it had taken so long to come rolling in. Of course she wouldn't be able to rest until she knew who her father was; met him, if he was still alive; rearranged her life along the guidelines which, trustingly, she felt he would show her, perhaps without knowing he was doing so. Only then, only with the peace of mind and the knowledge such a meeting would give, could she turn back to the two people she loved best in the world. It seems to me very wise of her, at seventeen, to realize that this was the way to finding and trusting them again; and she seems to have known it from the beginning: almost from the beginning, certainly from the moment the Drano had been poured into her mind, unblocking it.

As soon as she knew her mother was alone she went and asked her point-blank who her father really was. I can imagine the exact look in Ruth's gentle greenish eyes, almost a jade green: a cool and considering look; it was turned on me often enough at the time of my divorce. Marisa has inherited her beauty from her mother and her blue eyes from her maternal grandmother, Corinne: also some of her more sassy characteristics. It's a funny thing — this difference in eye color makes the two of them quite dissimilar; yet when you look carefully you can see Ruth's bone structure in her daughter; and these fine bones have enabled her to keep her looks past the witching age of forty: good news for Marisa. There are lines of course, but because there's been no surgical snipping and stretching they're virtually unnoticeable; and a touch of grey in fair hair is always attractive; some women pay the earth to have it put there.

She said, "Marisa, I'm not telling you who he is."

"Then he's alive."

"Yes. And he's a nice person, a good person. I didn't fall for a ski bum or a beach boy."

"Can't they be nice good people too?"

"Of course. You know what I mean." Was she touched by the glint of social conscience, a glint of rebellion in her child who had never given her any of the fashionable headaches, who thought drugs were strictly for dimwitted dropouts?

"So you fell for him and you had his baby, where did . . . where did Jack come in?"

"I already knew Jack. He . . . saved me from a very awkward situation, but that's the kind of person he is. As you know."

"Why didn't the man marry you?"

"He was already married."

"You could have got rid of me."

When Ruth gives you her straightest look you don't doubt her word: "I never, never for one moment thought of abortion, I promise you that. I wanted a child."

"His child."

"*My* child."

"Darn lucky you had Dad around."

Ruth was relieved to hear the 'Dad' and ignored the puerile sarcasm. Marisa knew better than to say outright, "I want to see him." In that respect, only apparent indifference could protect her, but she didn't find indifference easy to fake. She tried, "Haven't you got a picture of him?"

"No. How would your father like that?"

"He isn't my father; I wish he was. I wish you hadn't told me."

Ruth sighed and shook her head. "If you knew how we've argued. Argued, discussed, agreed, disagreed — around and around, never-ending."

"But you're glad you did it."

"It's a weight off my mind; I can't pretend it isn't."

"Off your mind and onto mine. You must have thought how it would be for me."

"Of course we did. But isn't the truth always better if . . . if it can be told?"

"No, lies are better."

"Oh my dear . . . " She held out her arms and Marisa let them enfold her. She intended to play this right. At the feel of those arms, which had always been there when she needed them, she felt the press of tears, but she was damned if she was going to cry in front of either of them. Tears were a form of acceptance, and she was accepting nothing.

Jack, home from another pre-production meeting, found her staring blankly out of her bedroom window. He said, "It doesn't *matter*, my dear, please try to see it that way. We've always loved you and we always will.

It's just . . . we couldn't bear cheating on you."

She looked at his handsome square face, tanned and healthy, curly hair graying at forty-seven, and said it again: "I'd rather be cheated. Maybe it's easier for you, it sure as hell isn't easier for me."

"But it was right. In the end you'll see that, and we'll all be . . . We'll be closer because of it."

"I hope so. What do I call you?"

"Oh for God's sake, Marisa, don't overplay it. You call me Dad, Father, just as you always have." She accepted the flash of impatient anger — he didn't suffer fools gladly; she admired that, it kept you on your toes; kept cameramen and actors, and more particularly wayward actresses, on their toes too. She could feel her love for him trapped inside her. OK, how was she going to let it out of the trap?

When he'd gone she raised her eyes and stared at the famous 'Hollywood' sign, deep in thought. As usual, a small

24

group of the faithful were toiling up Griffith Park towards it, and as usual a small group of guards had gathered to send them packing — in case any of them had fire, explosives, or even suicide in mind.

Like many other younger movie people touched by success, Jack and Ruth Adams had never even considered living in Beverly Hills, but had taken to the real hills of old Hollywood where so many of the old and great names had once lived. After them came the realtors and 'Hollywoodland'. How many of the devotees who regularly photographed one another with the sign in the background knew that this modern Mecca had been erected to advertise a housing development? And what did it matter in a town where fairy tales are all and the truth less than nothing? Lop off a last syllable and you have a myth.

So, gazing at 'Hollywood', Marisa wondered who would remember her mother's past, who would know? Well, for a start there was Ruth's own mother, Corinne. She would certainly know but, as certainly, would refuse to say; and would at once report to her daughter: "You've told her, haven't you? Nothing else could make her ask questions like that. What a mistake — why do you never listen to me?" Or something along those lines. Anyway she no longer lived in Los Angeles but had gone back to New York: "I know it may be dangerous but no more dangerous than LA, and at least it's *alive*." She was a jaunty old girl. When you're seventeen, sixty-six is a great age. No, Grandmother was out. Who then?

Seventeen years ago, or around then, her mother had been an actress, not, she often said, a very good one. Jack disagreed: she was good all right, but she'd never had the essential overriding ambition, and no chutzpah. Ruth invariably replied that in any case it was a matter of simple arithmetic: two show-biz careers into one family don't go. As for ambition and chutzpah, yes she must have lacked both because she was a happy woman.

Who would have known her in those days? Adult faces flitted through Marisa's mind, parental friends who had come and gone while she played house with Joanne under the bougainvillea on the other side of the pool — while she stood before the bedroom mirror wondering if she would ever reach sixteen. She hadn't even been interested in the ones who had since become famous.

But wait a minute! There was a couple who came to dinner every now and again. Hadn't they once been agents? Hadn't names flickered around the table? "Whatever happened to . . . ?" "Didn't you handle . . . ?" The kind of show-biz gossip which makes the young, if present, tune out. Sagging old faces, she could almost see them now. They must have been agents, they must have 'handled' Ruth Shallon, as she then was, or they wouldn't be friends, people who came to dinner as opposed to the rabble which attended the twice-yearly free-for-all around the pool. They had a Dutch name — Van-Something. Van-What? There couldn't be many Vs in the red book which lay beside the phone in the hall. There weren't, and there were only two Van-Anythings. The first lived in Amsterdam, the second was VanBuren, Henry and Barbara, Sunset Palisades. Marisa knew Sunset Palisades, one of her school friends lived out there in summer: nothing to do with the Boulevard, a new development way north of Malibu, north of Zuma: big houses on ledges, cleverly concealed one from the other by means of earth moving and skillful planting. Sounded kind of retired, but you could never be sure.

Was there still a VanBuren Agency? Yes there was, but a call confirmed that Henry and Barbara had sold out long ago, to the mega-operation Dermott-MacNally; they had probably been unable or perhaps unwilling to cope with the new Hollywood, which was really the old Hollywood wearing a different hat and a funny nose. OK, definitely retired. Now, how do you approach mother's old retired friends, almost certainly old agents, without setting off the jungle drums? You make up a story; doesn't have to be a good one, not in Southern California where anyone will believe anything, in fact crazy is better.

She found Henry and Barbara VanBuren next day, Friday, living in a splendid modern house with its feet, or anyway its private steps, in the ocean. Like many elderly people who have led active and interesting lives at the center of the whirlpool, they were bored to find themselves placidly rotating at its lazy outer edge. They had their golf, he had his fishing, she had her weaving (beautiful things), they both had their old friends, a few of whom like Ruth Adams had once been clients. Having met them, Marisa couldn't wait to get away from them, they depressed the hell out of her, and it was their careful politeness, eagerness to please the young in their old age, which depressed her most. Handsome, healthy, well-to-do old Californians, into their seventies with nowhere to go.

"You see," she heard herself saying, "I had this *great* idea. I should have done it on her fortieth but I guess her forty-second will be just as good." She intended to give her mother a surprise, a real *This is Your Life*, wasn't that a fabulous idea?

The VanBurens exchanged a quick glance which told her that they thought the idea less than fabulous, but they weren't about to hurt her feelings.

"And I wanted somebody who knew her way back when she was acting."

Gently they explained that of course they'd known Ruth in those ancient far-off days, she'd been their client and they adored her, but they were sure Marisa wouldn't mind if they, personally, opted out of this absolutely fantastic plan, *This is Your Life, Ruth Adams*. Too old, they hated to admit it — but of course they'd keep the secret, it sounded such a fun project.

Acting intense disappointment, Marisa said, "Well, perhaps you know someone else. Maybe some other actress, she must have had friends."

Henry VanBuren pounced on this like a drowning sailor bumping into a floating life-saver: "Barbie, who was that gal who brought Ruth around to the office — when she first came to town?"

Marisa wanted to shout, "Where from? Tell me where she came from," but that would have set the drums beating all right. She sat mute. "You remember, dear, Julie Something. They'd just made a picture together, hadn't they?"

"Oh yes." Barbara VanBuren's eyes congratulated him on finding this perfect escape. "You mean Julie Wrenn — I saw her in Hughes Market a couple of weeks ago." And to Marisa, benevolently, "An actress would be much more fun than a couple of old agents, she'd give you a real performance. And I bet your mother hasn't seen her in years. You're right, Henry — you clever old puss! — it was Julie Wrenn who introduced Ruth to the agency."

Before leaving them to their boredom, from which they hadn't even wanted to save themselves, Marisa again swore them to secrecy: it would all be spoiled if Ruth got so much as a hint of what was being planned. They stood together on their shining wraparound deck, with their expensive ocean view behind them, waving their bony, liver-spotted hands in farewell, and the breeze lifted their scanty white hair, showing the pink scalps beneath. Oh God, Marisa thought, turning back onto Pacific Coast Highway, save me from that, let me die young. Well, youngish.

★ ★ ★

She paused at this point, blue eyes inward turning on her thoughts. I noticed that she had taken something from her pocket and was holding it in one hand, touching it gently with the fingertips of the other. I said, "What's that?"

She smiled, revealing a piece of green soapstone carved into a toad, the kind of thing the Chinese turn out by the million. "Nick gave him to me."

Nick, drinking beer, said, "She's kinky that way."

"I always take him with me if I'm . . . you know, going to do something a bit way out."

"Like coming a thousand miles to look for Biological Dad."

"Right. He brings me luck."

Nick grimaced. "Didn't bring you much luck today."

Ignoring him she added, "He's called Cross-eye." She leaned towards me, a child suddenly, showing me how a fault in the stone did indeed make the little creature look cross-eyed. Then she put it back in her pocket. I remembered now that when I'd seen her at intervals over the years there had usually been some kind of talisman in her life: a round stone with a hole in it, found on the beach; an old one-dollar chip from Las Vegas; things like that. Now the toad. I said, "OK, we can eat." I carried the dish of pasta to the table; Nick followed with the salad; Marisa brought up the rear with hot French bread, two loaves — I'd remembered about teenage appetites.

Pouring wine, I asked, "Did you find this Julie Wrenn?"

"Did I ever!"

The lady had not been at home when Marisa first called; but she was at home on the Saturday morning, and she was every bit as dispiriting as the VanBurens but in a different way. It seems she had the kind of hangover which sticks out all around its owner like the horns of a naval mine — touch one and they explode. She lived in a shabby street off La Cienega near

Olympic Boulevard; immediately led the way out of the cramped little rented house onto an equally cramped patio where dead plants drooped in their pots, long unwatered: she probably knew the living room stank of booze and a sink full of dishes waiting to be washed. The sunlight made her wince and shade her eyes. "Ruth Shallon's kid, well I'll be darned! She should never have given it up — your dad being who he is, she'd be getting roles till she dropped."

Marisa couldn't see the *This is Your Life* angle going down too well with this defeated, once-pretty, maybe even once-slim bag of lard. Impossible to believe she must be roughly the same age as her mother; the difference was heart-rending. She sat down gingerly on a rather sticky lounger. Julie Wrenn kicked off her slippers and wiggled her toes; they were far from clean.

And Marisa had been right: in such a setting *This is Your Life, Ruth Adams* sounded surreal, but she played it to the hilt, deducting a couple of years from her age in the process. She wasn't sure Julie Wrenn even believed her, such pretty little excitements being so far, far outside the life to which she'd condemned herself. And the idea of her actually taking part in the mythical romp was grotesque — Marisa hastily added, "I mean, I'm not asking you to, you know, be in it. I just thought you could tell me someone who knew her back in her acting days. I mean she must have had agents, things like that."

"Batty old Barbara VanBuren. Saw her the other day in . . . I forget. Saw her anyway; she's still around."

Marisa said, "I've kind of heard of the VanBurens. Were they your agents too?"

"Long before they were hers. I introduced her." A touch of . . . what? Pride, combativeness, sagging into indifference.

"Of course! You made a movie together, didn't you?"

36

"She had a bit part. Local girl." She scratched between her sagging breasts. Marisa all but held her breath: would the oracle continue to speak? The oracle took a gulp of orange juice: "All I ever drink in the mornings. Want some?" Marisa could smell the vodka from where she was sitting. No orange juice for her, she didn't fancy using one of those smeared glasses.

"Sure we made a movie. Small budget. Your dad's first."

A piece fell into place. ('He saved me from a very awkward situation.')

"Can't remember the title, something about a wagon. Total bummer. I wonder he ever got another job, let alone . . . " A wave of the grubby fingers sketched the upward trajectory of Jack Adams. "Luck of the draw, dear, that's what they call it. All about the pioneers coming to Oregon. Crap, arty crap. Didn't do me a blind bit of good. I played the daughter, nice part."

Marisa sat very still, not even daring to look at the woman. She said,

"Oregon's beautiful, isn't it?"

"Kind of quiet, but . . . yeah, it's beautiful." Oh God, she seemed to have come to a stop. Or maybe just searching her pickled memory for names: "The Columbia. And that other river, what's it called? Runs through Portland."

Marisa felt that too many questions might seem suspicious, might dam the flow; but questions had to be asked. "Did you . . . Did you like Portland?"

"It's OK. Better than this asshole city ever was, even in its good days."

A local girl. Portland, Oregon. She could hardly believe how much she'd managed to discover in so short a time. Jack Adams' first movie had been something about a wagon, about pioneers coming to the West. An arty failure. This pathetic woman had played the daughter, and her mother, the local girl, had been given a bit part. How come? Obvious — she'd been an actress up there in Portland; sometimes she spoke about acting on the stage, but she had never done it in LA, therefore it must have been in Portland. And if the wagon movie was being made on a small budget they would have depended on local talent, would have visited the theaters to find it, had found Ruth Shallon.

And when shooting was finished she had left Oregon to come to LA — to hide her pregnancy? — just another out-of-town girl trying to make the big time; and Julie Wrenn had introduced her to the VanBuren Agency. How did things then stand between the young actress and the young director?

Sitting there in that dreadful desolate patio, Marisa realized what thin, thin ice they'd been walking on, those two loved people. As a child of Hollywood she knew very well what would have happened if the media had caught the faintest whiff of what was going on. Young actress, pregnant by another man, sets her sights on up-and-coming young director and brings it off. The fact that this not-unheard-of scenario sounded laughable when applied to

Ruth and Jack made her suddenly proud of them. Perhaps, unknown to her, pride was the first step in coming to terms with the hurtful truth.

Yet even while she thought of them with pride and love, that determination still urged her on: she must talk to her true father, she must 'feel his genes' in her; that was her way towards the light at the end of the tunnel, the light in which she would find peace and happiness again.

But right now she knew that she had to keep Oregon in Julie Wrenn's mind, or vodka would take over, destroying the whole chain of thought: a rusty chain, many links no doubt missing. She said, "Pity the movie was a bummer. But it must have been a fun location."

The eyes which were raised to hers already had that soggy, dulled look. "What location? Oh . . . Portland." The regard sharpened somewhat. "Hooked on that, aren't you? What are you after?"

"I thought . . . thought maybe I could find a couple of Mom's old buddies from up there. For the birthday thing." She could see that this detail had also been forgotten. "You know — like I told you . . . "

"Oh sure, *This is Your Life*."

"People she hadn't seen for years — that would really be a surprise, wouldn't it?"

A sly glance. "Too much maybe."

"How d'you mean?"

"Could dig up the wrong ones, couldn't you? Old boyfriends. Your dad wouldn't like that."

Marisa's heart lurched. Her mouth seemed to have dried up. She couldn't find words to unearth this buried gold; managed, "Oh. I hadn't . . . thought of that. How would I know?"

"For a start, honey, you can avoid the name Hartman."

"Was that . . . a boyfriend?"

"*The* boyfriend, I heard tell." She waved her glass, vodka and orange slurping. "Oh Christ, I'm being a bitch. Who knows, who cares? It was a thousand years ago; it's her business, not mine, not yours."

Marisa's heart was thudding so hard that it seemed to be shaking her whole body. Hartman — it might be *exactly* her business. "Was he . . . ? I mean, was he a serious boyfriend?"

"I don't know. Rich as hell . . . Forget it." She reached for her jug of orange juice and managed to change the subject with an almost audible grinding of gears. "Matter of fact, your mom and I did another movie together. Down in New Mexico, what's the place called, hell hole? *Stranger in Town*, good movie. Harold Gage directed . . . " Marisa could see that the oracle had no intention of returning to Oregon. And she'd better get away before all kinds of random reminiscences began piling up like rush-hour traffic, the way they did at her parents' dinner parties. But in fact New Mexico had been a small bonus — she'd been born in New Mexico: Santa Fe.

In reply to her polite thanks and goodbye, Julie Wrenn merely nodded, at the same time refilling her glass. Marisa went home, clutching her golden nugget: Hartman — *the* boyfriend. What next? A year ago she might have gone storming up to Portland right away, but at the ripe age of seventeen she took a shower, lay on her bed for a while, and came to the conclusion that some kind of confirmation was called for. Ruth had never mentioned the Oregon connection; this in itself was a negative confirmation — she'd hardly mention it if she had things to hide.

Marisa rolled off her bed, pulled on jeans and a T-shirt and went down the hall to the small room known as Mother's Den. Mother was out, Marisa had checked the cars. The room was cool and pleasant, facing north. A Japanese couple were teetering at the top of the steep bank which fell away from the Adams property; they were trying to get the 'Hollywood' sign behind their heads before their friends took the photograph. If they weren't careful they'd go slithering down the crumbling hillside and find themselves at the mercy of spiny yucca, all kinds of cruel thorns, maybe poison oak.

In the bottom drawer of Ruth's desk there was a pretty red and gold book which came out of hiding in November: 'Christmas Cards'. Only three days ago Marisa would never have dreamed of poking around among her mother's private belongings. She thumbed through the neat pages and almost immediately stumbled over Koskela, Beth, who lived in Beaverton, an extension of Portland, Oregon; and here were Greg and Kathy Nelson of Oregon City, no less; and here also was Lina Thomassen of Eugene, Oregon. (And yes, of course, here was her one-time Uncle Will: a long list of deleted addresses, a wanderer over the face of the earth: at present roosting in Astoria, Oregon — maybe he'd be getting a visitor before very long.) She found several more Oregon addresses — no other state was so well represented; the name, Hartman, was conspicuous by its absence — not a negative omission, in Marisa's opinion, but a positive one. So Julie Wrenn's bibulous evidence was partly confirmed, the Oregon connection certainly existed.

What next? Next she called her friend Nick Deering, and got an earful.

★ ★ ★

Her friend Nick Deering pushed his plate away — they'd both eaten two enormous helpings of pasta — and said, "I'll say she got a earful, why not?" He was a good listener, rare at any age, even more so at seventeen, and only spoke when he had something to add, as now: "For God's sake, I'd called her a hundred times, I was shit scared. I mean, this was Saturday, and on Thursday night she'd been next thing to suicidal."

"Thursday night seemed like another world."

"Great. All you had to do was tell me."

She put a hand over his. "I'm sorry." Nick looked at me. "Then she calls and says she has to go up to Oregon."

"And he shouts *Oregon* as if I'd said Botswana."

"Sure. I thought you'd gone crazy — with school starting Monday and both of us supposed to get top grades."

I grabbed this one: "Yes, what about school? I'm a dad from way back, remember? It's been worrying me."

Marisa nodded. "Worries me too."

"Considering what your folks pay," said Nick, "it should." And to me, "I'm good old Hollywood High, pushers' paradise." He looked as if he could take it. Ruth and Jack wouldn't even consider it for their daughter; they reckoned just growing up was a big enough problem for a girl without that; and anyway they had the money for a private education. I knew it was no time to be going on about school; I said, "So where are we now? Day

46

before yesterday, right?"

Nick replied, "Right — Saturday evening. We started north on Sunday. Had to wait until her folks were out of the way."

"Brunch," added Marisa. "All that poolside crap, out at Bel Air. They weren't surprised I wouldn't go, I never do. So we started late and had to spend Sunday night in Medford. Hit Portland around noon today."

"Hit being operative," said Nick. "Or did it hit us?"

Marisa had been sure that as soon as she saw the Portland phone directory she'd find her Hartman; she was wrong. Several Hartmans, yes, but their addresses didn't add up to being 'rich as hell', Julie Wrenn's words.

Nick said, "Figures. Rich-as-hell people have unlisted numbers."

They had brooded over this for a while. He was all for continuing their journey to Astoria, finding not-Uncle Will and enlisting his help; she, spurred by her 'Sherlocking' successes in LA,

47

felt that a little application, a little tenacity, would still lead them to a male Hartman who was not only rich but about the right age to have been her mother's lover seventeen years before. What age? Probably older than Ruth who had been twenty-four; maybe a man of around thirty, now around forty-seven.

It was when even Marisa had all but abandoned hope — when they were driving through downtown Portland to pick up Interstate 5 — that they both saw it, at exactly the same moment: 'Hartman', written house-high in aggressive steel lettering against the sky: a big new building, some twenty-five floors of it, dominating its neighbors with self-assured power. The surprise made them both laugh; Marisa said, "There he is, that's him!"

They parked opposite the building — no easy task: it took a half-hour and involved four circuits of the downtown area — then walked across the street to look at it. A palatial sweep of steps led up to massive steel doors, six of them, which flashed in the sun every time anyone went in or out. Beyond the doors was an enormous atrium carpeted in acres of scarlet, and on either side of them were two ever-changing display systems which informed the world that Hartman was transportation, including airlines; was oil; was hydroelectric power; was software and timber, steel and mining, hotels and real estate. While they were staring, a group of young men in suits emerged from the place laughing and joshing; some of them went across the street to Steve's Espresso. Marisa and Nick followed. Unsurprisingly, she never has difficulty in finding young men who are happy to talk to her. One, Adrian, natty in dark grey with a subdued tie, junior exec. personified, proved to be a mine of information. Oh God, yes, Hartman was money all right; Hartman had been money around here for a hundred and fifty years. Those goodies shown on the display were only the tip of the iceberg — OK, call it the acceptable tip — you could add anything you cared to think of and you'd probably be right.

It appeared that the existing Hartman wasn't too interested in the source of his wealth, hardly ever put in an appearance over the road. But that was what big money was for, wasn't it? The ultimate liberating factor. Clearly young Adrian himself couldn't wait for the seniority which would ultimately liberate him. Right now he had to go, business was business, but (a cautious glance at Nick, twice his size) if Marisa wanted to know more they could meet some evening . . . Marisa hugged Nick's arm and said she was sorry, that wouldn't be possible. The junior exec. personified withdrew.

She said, "I'm going in there. I've a hunch we've hit the jackpot."

Nick was less sure. "What are you going to say?"

"Final year's project — big business, how it works. What better place to find

50

out than Hartman Inc.?"

He said, as he'd said many times before, "Marisa, think first for Christ's sake."

"No. Sound, camera, *action*!"

"You have to be kidding."

"Watch me."

And watch he did, as she crossed the street, stood gazing at one of the displays until a gaggle of secretaries approached the doors, then joined them and disappeared from sight. Nick knew that he tended to be overly cautious by nature, but he couldn't ignore the sinking feeling in his stomach.

Inside the atrium, which seemed to stretch upwards to infinity, Marisa trekked across a mile of scarlet carpet until she reached the information desk. To the expertly painted lady behind it she explained this pregraduation project which was so important to her final grades: an in-depth portrait of big business doing its thing. So, nothing ventured nothing gained, she immediately thought of Hartman — why not aim for the top, right? Why not even try to get fifteen minutes with boss Hartman himself?

The painted lady gave this careful thought. The girl confronting her was no weirdo; she was educated, bright and beautiful, and she was wearing cashmere slung carelessly around her shoulders, and that meant class, beware. For a start, she replied, it wouldn't actually be possible to see Mr Scott Hartman, he hadn't set foot in the office for a long, long time. Of course Hartman Inc. was always very conscious of its public image . . .

Marisa hadn't been aware of the arrival of a tall young man in glasses; suddenly he was at the other end of the desk — and interested. The painted lady said, "I'm sure Publicity would help you." Marisa wasn't sure how far she should push her man-at-the-top request; but she still had a strong feeling that Mr Scott Hartman was the one she'd come all this way to find, and she wasn't altogether sure that she wouldn't in the end find him right here in a resplendent office on the twenty-fifth floor. It's very easy, even if you're not seventeen and relatively inexperienced, to imagine you're moving events along your chosen route when, in fact, events are actually moving in a quite different direction of which you know nothing; reality seldom pays much attention to one's wishes.

The man in glasses said, "Perhaps I could help."

"Oh, Mr Rineman, would you? This is Miss . . ."

"Allison, Mary Allison." It seemed wise to start off with a false name.

"Mr Harry Rineman, one of our publicity directors."

Mr Rineman was fair and balding, with a thin bony face and sharp, pale blue eyes. Marisa noticed the eyes but, euphoric in her Sherlocking mood, didn't pay them the attention they deserved.

"Stay right here," he said, "while I ask a few questions."

He returned inside ten minutes and said, "Great. Why don't we go to my office, and I can make a note of the kind of things you'd like to know. A school project, I think you said."

Yes, but Marisa was pretty sure he hadn't been there when she'd said it. This thought induced a flash of uneasiness which the office did nothing to ameliorate; it was large, even luxurious, but it had no windows. Mr Rineman asked for particulars of her school. Marisa knew she should have expected this and worked out a story; she remembered Nick's words of wisdom, "Think first for Christ's sake." Now, for lack of forethought, she had to give the name of her real school.

"Oh. In LA!"

"Yes, my mom went there, she wanted me to follow on."

She was saved from further improvisation by the appearance of a large young man: handsome, tanned, with greedy-looking lips and cold grey eyes — and an air of absolute authority.

He said, "I'm told you were asking for Scott Hartman in person. Why?" No smooth politeness here; he was to the point, and harsh with it. And why the 'in person', how else could she have asked for anyone by name? Feeling less sure of herself, she repeated the story of her pregraduation project; it was beginning to sound flimsy.

Authority said, "But why Mr Hartman?"

"He . . . He seemed the biggest big businessman around."

"There are plenty just as big in California."

"Sure. But . . . I happened to be here, visiting."

"School went back this morning, and your school's in LA." How did he know that, he hadn't been in the room? The place must be wired. She began to feel very uneasy indeed, aware of the situation nose-diving out of control; she wasn't sure how or why: naturally, because she had no idea of the real direction she'd been taking ever since she entered the building.

Greedy-lips came closer; he was overpowering — sexy, she felt that in her gut, but also violent. The grey eyes examined her as if she were a slug found among the petunias. "I think you're lying, giving us a load of baloney. You're media, aren't you? Who do you work for?" She usually enjoyed being thought older than her years, but not this time. "I don't work for anyone, I'm nothing to do with — "

He turned from her abruptly and said, "Rineman, keep her here. I want to make a couple of inquiries."

Keep her here. This was when Marisa panicked; but with the panic came the certain knowledge that she must remain cool. She said to Publicity, "Who's he?"

"I'm sure he'll tell you himself. If he wants you to know." The pale blue eyes were no longer friendly; they reminded her of a school friend's Siamese cat, an avaricious killer of mice and small birds. Why the hell did she never listen to Nick? He was so damned sensible. Obviously she had to get the hell out of here before Greedy-lips returned. But how? Mr Rineman was standing purposefully in front of the only door. Panic began to swell inside her; she felt it might at any moment escape in a high-pitched scream. And her brain wasn't operating again. Where was the Drano?

Ever since entering this creepy office she'd been clutching Cross-eye, her soapstone toad; she was just wondering whether he was going to turn out to be a dead loss when he summoned chance to her aid. It arrived in the shape of a secretary who pushed open the door without knocking and dealt Mr Publicity Director Rineman a sharp blow on the back of his balding head. The secretary, a frantic blonde and, by the look of her, a dumbbell, launched into strenuous apology, at the same time trying not to drop the teetering tower of folders she was carrying. "Oh Mr Rineman, oh I'm so — "

He had stepped away from the door willy-nilly, and was now stretching out both hands to catch some of the folders as they began to spill onto the floor, scattering loose pages. Marisa darted behind the girl's back into a corridor, into the vast atrium. Things then happened very quickly and in no recognizable order. Mr Rineman was undoubtedly shouting somewhere behind her, maybe Greedy-lips as well. A few passers-by gaped, others passed hurriedly by. The lady at Information was staring, brows raised. Marisa ran as fast as she could towards the heavy steel doors, sure that she'd find them electronically locked. Not so — they even opened for her as she approached. A man in uniform, Security, no doubt, was by then turning towards her, but she was already at the top of the steps; went leaping down them; saw a gap in the traffic and darted across the street to a fanfare of horns.

Nick had seen her and was staring open-mouthed. He flung himself into her Subaru station wagon as she reached it; a second later she was beside him and they were moving; and — oh God! — lights at the end of the block were changing to red. Looking in the mirror she saw, as Nick had evidently also seen, a couple of Hartman security men closing in on them.

Nick said, "Oh Christ!" as Marisa shot the lights. More horns, a screech of burning rubber. But they'd made it.

"Hm!" was all I could say when she'd finished. I was thinking that none of it had been exactly clever, but on the other hand I found her devil-may-care courage rather endearing.

Nick said, "'Hm!' just about nails it."

"And after this . . . " I was aware of sounding like a prosecuting attorney. "After this you were forced off the road."

Marisa was sure it had nothing to do with the drama at Hartman.

"How could it, Will? I mean, this guy suddenly appears out of left-field . . . "

"Like," I said, "Mr Rineman."

She stared at me. "Nobody could have picked up on us that quick."

"I go with Will — Mr Rineman did." Nick was cutting himself another chunk of French bread and buttering it. Marisa looked at it longingly. He divided it and gave her half.

"No," she said. "The guy was smashed, he was making a pass at me, you know how they are."

It seems that this big pick-up, towering on mountain wheels, materialized in the fast lane, swerving in towards the Subaru. "Honestly," she said, "it looked a mile high, I could hardly see the driver." A second later the pick-up had closed again, and there was a scream of metal as it sheared along the side of the station wagon. No one else paid any attention: minding their own business, the modern virtue.

Nick said, "Jesus it was scary, those huge tires!"

By this time Marisa's offside wheels were scrabbling along the rough shoulder, and her car was yawing to and fro, gravel flying.

"She was great," said Nick. "I saw the turn-off coming before she did, and I was pointing and yelling — and just as the bastard came swerving in again she wrenched the wheel over and zing, he was gone. Trapped on the freeway, see, while we shot off into Something-or-other Avenue."

They were completely lost, but at least they were free of the maniac's attentions. How far it was to the next turn-off was anyone's guess, but by then he might have forgotten them, if he was indeed drunk; if on the other hand he was still interested it would take him a long time to reach the spot where they'd evaded him, whether he rejoined the freeway in the opposite direction or tried to make his way back by residential side streets. They drove off into the hinterland, found a mini-market and bought themselves a much-needed Coke. Half an hour later they returned to the freeway, via another entrance.

Once or twice during the next hour they were sure they were being followed — which was why Nick had taken so long parking when they finally reached Astoria; he wanted to make sure it had only been their imagination.

Well, I thought, there were plenty of good reasons for all that nervous tension; some kids I'd known would have been in need of first aid. I said, "Hartman. I wonder why they were so touchy."

"They thought I was a media person."

"OK. Why so touchy about the media? And how about the guy in the pick-up?"

"I still don't think he was anything to do with them."

"Coincidence, eh?"

Nick shook his head; clearly he didn't

believe in coincidence either. We all considered the situation in silence. Then I said, "What do you want to do next, Marisa?"

"I just have this feeling he's it, I don't know why."

Nick added, "I just have this feeling we could do with some help from not-Uncle Will."

"We might dream up a more subtle way of going about it." I smiled to blunt the sharp adult edge. "For a start it may be true he's never in that office; I think we have to find out where he lives. And even if Ms Julie Wrenn was right, we'd better make sure he wasn't just *a* boyfriend. He doesn't have to be biological Dad."

She nodded, accepting this. Nick relaxed a little; it was obviously what he'd been hoping I'd say. I could understand that being the sole curb on Marisa's impulses might well be exhausting, particularly if you were no older than she was.

The blue eyes were very direct. "Are

you going to help me?"

"How, is the question. Let me think it over."

The wind blustered and hurled buckets of Oregon rain at the windows, a cozy sound as long as you're safe indoors. I could see that their heroic day, not to mention the thousand-mile drive preceding it, not to mention the large meal they'd just consumed, were all taking their toll; they were only managing to keep their eyes open because it would have been impolite to let them close. I suggested we make up the bed; we could talk some more in the morning, and by then I might have come up with an idea. There were no disagreements. As a matter of fact I'd already had the idea, but sudden inspiration should never be voiced until it's been allowed to marinate for a while, preferably overnight; ideas often lead to further ideas.

Bed-making was weird and wonderful; they preferred to sleep head to toe. "In case," she said, "he kind of half wakes up and thinks I'm a boy."

"Nobody," replied her best friend, taking the words out of my mouth, "could possibly mistake you for a boy."

Myself, I didn't feel sleepy: too many questions weaving around in my mind, most of them requiring answers from Ruth, some from my brother Jack. What worried me most was the thought of their gnawing anxiety. Would they have put the police onto their daughter? Probably not yet, possibly not ever, even if they wanted to: there were enough wounds to be healed without that one. Did they know that she'd taken off with Nick? He was only a youngster but evidently a prudent and resourceful youngster, and that would be some comfort.

My first loyalty was to Jack and Ruth of course, and yet there was something about their daughter's dogged independence which also demanded loyalty. I would have to tell them she was with me and safe (relatively speaking) but I could only do so after she'd agreed that it must be done: a weak decision certainly, but what in life is weaker than divided loyalty, and what more common?

Had anyone asked me earlier that evening if I loved my brother I would have replied, "No, not really." I admired him, yes, and occasionally enjoyed his company, in small doses; but sibling love has always struck me as being either a very strong emotion, or a thing you take for granted and ignore. So I was surprised to find that now, a few hours later, my answer would have been different; perhaps there's more feeling between us than I've ever supposed.

The fact is he'd become remote: a noted figure occasionally seen on television, accepting some award with a witty little speech. Misfortune seemed to have snapped him back into focus. What a heart-wrenching thing to have to do, telling that loved child he wasn't her real father. His marriage, in a town of nonmarriages, has always been considered perfect; both he and Ruth are honest and honorable people — it's a wonder he ever made it in that dishonest, perfidious industry.

I suppose that always, from the start, they'd meant to tell Marisa the truth; and knowing Ruth as I did, I was sure it wasn't a very shameful truth. Presumably they'd put it off and put it off, trying to decide what age would be the right one. Not this year, she's just a kid. Maybe next year, they grow up so quickly. And then Ruth had again become pregnant; had they convinced themselves that presently, when Marisa had a small brother, things would become easier?

Easier! It seems incredible in our world, and in that city of prestigious hospitals, but something went disastrously wrong. One day it appeared to be a normal pregnancy with five weeks to go, next day it was the emergency ward and an oxygen tent. Ruth nearly died and, thank God, a decision was made not to save the baby, which had suffered brain damage during delivery. It was six weeks before Ruth recovered sufficiently to be told she could never have another child.

So there was only Marisa, and how infinitely precious she must then have seemed. Did they really have to tell her? Supposing it turned her against them? And there the agonizing indecision had stayed, a cancer of untruth in the minds of two honest people: until a dinner-party argument had tipped the scales — we all know those scales, they take very little tipping.

Marisa came out of the bathroom and padded over to where I was sitting. In pajamas, hair tousled, she looked twelve years old again, beautiful eyes clouded by sleep and, it seemed, by doubt: "Will, those things I did, were they wrong?"

Moral sense is always touching. I said, "Right, wrong, who knows? Who cares, as long as you get yourself straightened out and happy again?"

She smiled and kissed my cheek. I

went with her to the bedroom door and looked in. "Sound asleep. I bet you sleep sound too. Get up when you feel like it — I'll be out, got to see to my boat."

"You have a boat?"

"Last time I looked. Weather like this, she may be at the bottom of the river by now, she's an old lady."

Her eyes were closing as she stood there. Mine didn't close for a long time: continuing mental indigestion.

3

I can't discover the origins of *Mary Celeste II*, but whoever christened her had a dark sense of humor. You may recall that in 1872 the brigantine *Mary Celeste* (I) was found off the Azores, bowling along under half-sail with no one on board, not a soul; the captain, his wife and baby daughter, and a crew of seven were never heard of again. Dozens of explanations have been suggested over the years, from drunken mutiny — the cargo was commercial alcohol, but it would have killed anyone who drank it — to sea monsters, plague and waterspouts. Conan Doyle announced that the tea in the galley was still warm and breakfast was cooking — absolutely untrue. It remains one of the great mysteries of the sea.

Mary Celeste II is a twenty-foot cabin cruiser, of sorts, with a stumpy mast and no sail. She is steered, not by a nice tidy wheel in the cabin but by an old-fashioned tiller. (Does this indicate that she was once a sailing boat?) When you're at the tiller the engine hatch, under which reposes a bloody-minded old diesel, is at your feet, so you can control her speed by leaning forward and dealing with this machine directly, an unusual procedure. Such arcane details make her an object of amusement; and so does her figure; she's tubby, and it looks as though successive owners arrived at her present eccentric shape by adding bits and pieces whenever they felt the urge. I'm not sure how far she'd sail with no one on board, but she can potter very agreeably to and fro on the Columbia, as long as I keep her well away from the infamous bar where river and ocean collide, and where many ships a hundred, two hundred, times her size have come to grief. I've described her at some length because she plays a role in this story, and one not unworthy of her notorious name.

I bought her from the man who was moving out of the apartment when I moved in: bought her for a song, which is all I could afford and maybe all she's worth. I love her dearly. Greg Johansen, who owns the small marina on the Skipanon River where I keep her, is fond of her too. On that particular morning he wouldn't let me take her out of the water — or more properly wouldn't take her out of the water for me — because, he said, once this wind had blown itself out we'd be having an indian summer: perfect weather for *Mary Celeste* and me to go pottering. As a result I left her where she was, one of those negative decisions which have positive consequences.

When I got back to the house, which contains three large apartments on its three floors, I saw that Andy Swensen was cleaning the panes of glass in and around the grandiose front door. My heart fell because he only does this job, very badly, when he feels talkative, waylaying any hapless tenant who needs to enter or exit. I suppose I have to describe him because he too, like *Mary Celeste*, is important to what follows. He's supposed to be our caretaker, but since the apartments are entirely self-contained, each having its own central and water heating, there's nothing much for him to do except keep the front and back yards tidy and flourishing; he doesn't like gardening, or any other form of physical labor, so they're always neglected. He lives, with a mountainous wife, too fat to move, in the basement; this is by no means as bad as it sounds because the house is on a steep slope, and at the back his windows offer all the light in the world and a fine view of the river. He's the half-brother of the owner, who resides in a squalid mobile home in the middle of a field about ten miles out of town, making a small fortune from our combined rents.

When I'd run the gauntlet, declining to gossip — I knew I'd pay for it; Andy can be spiteful — I found Marisa sitting at the table in the bay window admiring the view. Showered and dressed and as fresh as a violet, she was eating toast and butter and apricot jam. Nick was singing 'Shenandoah' in the bathroom. It was nice, for a while anyway, and chapter nine notwithstanding, to have youngsters around again; I knew a sudden pang for my solitary state in life — brought on, of course, by myself.

"So," she said, "how was your boat?"

"As dotty as ever." I had a feeling that in more normal times she'd have been asking for a day afloat (I didn't then know she was afraid of water) but these weren't normal times, and there was only one thing on her mind. She waited until I'd helped myself to coffee before saying, "How do I find him, Will? Where do I start?"

I'd known last night exactly where she could start: with a very sharp lady who lived in a large old house in Portland, Connie Sherwood King. But during the night this idea had spawned another, as I'd hoped it would: Connie was a powerful card, and I wasn't about to play her without taking at least one trick; so I replied, "OK Marisa, let's deal. I'll help you start your quest, if you let me call your mother and tell her you're all right."

While she was considering this, blue eyes fixed on a piece of toast, Nick came out of the bathroom. Marisa transferred her gaze to her best friend. "Will wants to deal. He'll help me if I let him call home."

"Depends how good the help's going to be, doesn't it?" The generations were once again locked — he reminded me of my son, Harry.

Marisa said, "He's right. How good is the help going to be?"

"I have up my magical sleeve a lady who knows everything that's gone on in and around Portland for the last forty years, and I mean everything."

"Then she'd know rich-as-hell Mr Hartman."

"Certainly. If he exists." I thought it better not to add that Connie would only divulge what she knew after her prodigious memory had scrutinized it with extreme care; her middle name was Diplomacy. She was 'old money' herself — except that her father had spent it all.

"Would she know about Dad's first movie, the bummer?"

"Of course."

"How come?"

"She used to be a journalist, she wrote *the* social page for umpteen years."

They considered this for a while, and

we all gazed out of the window. The Washington hills, rising to mountains, were rain-washed and sparkling clear: too clear, it's never a good sign. Tremendous cumuli were sailing in majestically from the northwest where the Pacific builds its most magnificent clouds, and their shadows came sliding, undulating towards us: down the forested slopes and into the Columbia, turning it from icy blue to an ominous purple-gray, against which two tugs, coaxing a vast barge upriver towards Longview, remained dramatically sunlit. I never tire of this ever-changing panorama and have to work with my back to it.

Marisa said to Nick, "What do you think?"

"I think you should go for it."

Marisa nodded and finished the toast; then, eyes fixed on me over her coffee: "For a start you'd better know I laid a false trail. Unless I screwed it up they think I've gone south — to New Mexico, Santa Fe."

"Clever old you."

76

"I don't know. They're not silly." A shrug. "If you call her she'll be on the next plane."

"Probably."

She glanced at her watch and said, "OK, it's a deal." Even the glance at the watch had a meaning, as I was to discover in a minute; it told her that the time was 9.40 and the date the 6th, Tuesday. I went to the phone, found the number in my book and tapped it out. If I knew Ruth she'd be sitting at the other end of the line, anxiously waiting. In fact as soon as I heard a woman's voice I said, "Ruth?" even as I realized it wasn't Ruth.

"No, this Luanne. Mrs Adams out, Mr Adams studio."

I pressed the mute button and said to Marisa, "Luanne. Want to speak to her?" She shook her head. I told Luanne I'd call again later.

With some satisfaction, Marisa said, "She's never home 9.40, Tuesday morning. Tennis."

OK, game to the little girl, set and

match still to be played. I couldn't see Ruth frisking off to the tennis club in the middle of a crisis, but anyway . . . I said, "When does she get back?"

"Around noon."

"Then I'm calling her at noon."

Looking even more pleased with herself, she said, "But right now we get on with your side of the deal."

"I guess." I suppose if one's going to be conned, it might as well be by a pretty girl.

My call to Connie Sherwood King in Portland was more productive, she even sounded pleased to hear from me again. "Sure," she said, "come on by. Any time before a quarter of one, I have a luncheon." 'Luncheon' was pretty darned good; I hadn't heard anyone in Oregon, and few in the United States, use it.

I said to Nick, "Better take both cars."

"Why?" asked Marisa.

"Because if your mother decides to fly up here immediately I'm going to have to meet her."

She got it in one. "And then you'll want to talk like grown-ups, right?"

"Right."

"With me out of earshot."

"Right."

She caught Nick's eye and received some kind of signal which I couldn't unscramble. He said, "Good idea really, and Portland's only just up the road."

I suppose it's the British side of me which can never think of a ninety-mile drive as 'just up the road'. Ninety, a hundred and ninety, nine hundred and ninety miles, the Americans in their vast country think nothing of it; their cars are extensions of their bodies. To me, a car is just a pain in what they sometimes call the butt. As soon as we left the house, the dreaded Andy Swensen popped up from behind the privet hedge which separates us from our neighbors. I can never decide whether he looks worse with his few hairs carefully draped over his bald head or with them trailing over his left ear, as now. He was armed with a pair of clippers, but if he'd been using them on the hedge there was no sign of it.

He gazed after us while we went to the vacant lot next door where the tenants park their cars; it is edged with brambles and old laurels, with even a rose or two left over from the days when a house had stood there. He was eying the two youngsters with lip-smacking curiosity, clearly trying to calculate which of them I'd lured into my bed. Or maybe even a threesome! My single state fascinates him, and his wife is obsessed by it; she's one of those prurient sacks of fat who are forever reading the *Sun* and the *Examiner*, and making inaccurate predictions about other people's sexual habits. My predecessor had warned me about her.

I'm sure he was delighted to see me get into my Taurus with Marisa, while Nick sat behind the wheel of her Subaru station wagon alone. He abandoned the pretence of hedging and went to report to the fat lady.

Marisa was sitting with me because I'd realized we had to get our story together before presenting it to Mrs Sherwood King. I said, "You're not an illegitimate child searching for its father, and you're not planning to surprise Mom with *This is Your Life*. So?"

"Surprising Mom isn't bad, Will. It kind of leaves things open. How about a surprise birthday party? People do it all the time. A surprise party and I want to invite a few of her old buddies from Portland. People she acted with way back when. And maybe her old friend, Mr Hartman, too."

I said, "Marisa, I don't think we mention Hartman; we'd only be putting the name into her head. Let's see if she comes up with one of her own — it could be the answer."

"I think Hartman's the answer." But all the same she saw the sense of what I'd said, and added, "OK, we'll just hang the party on her, and see what gives."

Since Connie was an American I supposed the idea of dragging friends a thousand miles for a celebration would seem ordinary, like ninety miles being 'just up the road'. They may have their faults — who doesn't? — but by and large, and to an extent no European can really assimilate, they think big.

Marisa added, "Would she believe it?"

I said that Mrs Sherwood King's belief was beside the point as long as our story was what the French call *convenable*: untranslatable, like all the good French words, but meaning something like 'believable if one doesn't wish to examine it too closely'. I thought it would do, and the surprise angle would explain why teenage daughter was asking questions behind Mother's back.

The two of them were pretty impressed by Connie's house; I was always pretty impressed myself, at the same time wondering why Edwardian ebullience, considered tacky or worse in England, should seem properly grand and not at all out of place in the Willamette valley. Something to do with money and, again, thinking big — it had ten bedrooms.

Nick said, "And this lady lives here alone!"

I explained that since giving up her career as a columnist Connie had embarked on a much more profitable one as proxy-hostess and arranger of other people's festivities. The house still saw many a coming-out or anniversary celebration, and could even be rented in its entirety if ten bedrooms were required for visiting guests: expensive, I had no doubt, but a fraction of what a generous host would have to shell out for hotel accommodation of the same standing. American society is deftly compartmentalized; the kind of stately free-for-all held in this small palace would be of little interest to most 'ordinary people'; they have their own lives to cope with, just as important if not more so. Money and position are respected and sometimes envied, but not in, for instance, the British manner where an entire population can behave like housemaids gazing up out of the kitchen basement as wealth and station trundle by in their carriages. To that extent, at least, the United States is a great republic.

Marisa said, "How come you know her, Will?"

"I'm writing a book which covers sixty years of life around here. She's helped me more than anyone else, she's quite an historian on the side."

Constance Sherwood King invariably wears little expensive black suits, Chanel-type suits. She isn't tall, but a well-kept figure and expertise with high heels, something many modern women lack, make her look elegant and distinguished. Her small head is distinguished anyway; she has worn her white hair, white since youth, in the same short bob all her life. She readily admits she was never beautiful: the readiness of a woman who long ago proved to herself that character, and in former years sex appeal, are as effective as beauty.

The house is full of good furniture and some fine pictures procured by her grandmother, also by her mother before Father's disastrous speculations exhausted the money. In spite of this crash, very little seems to have been sold; you have to respect that sort of family pride.

I think perhaps Connie genuinely likes me; she is too much of a lady to show dislike, but on the other hand she's too much herself to pretend affection if it doesn't exist. She eyed the two youngsters with wary humor, deploring the way they were dressed no doubt — such a waste of a beautiful girl — but long used to it. Over coffee and what I'm sure she'd have called *petits fours*, I explained the mythical birthday party and the desire to resurrect some of Mother's old friends to attend it.

Had she by any chance known Mother in the days when she'd been an actress in Portland — it would have been in the seventies.

"What did you say her name is?"

Marisa said, "It's Ruth Adams now. My . . . my father's Jack Adams, the director."

"Really! I thought *Returning Woman* quite excellent; adult movies are rare. What was your mother's name when she was here?"

"Shallon. Ruth Shallon."

A nod. "In the seventies, you say. The name does . . . kind of ring a bell. I was doing my column then; I'll have to look at the file."

Now this is a very professional lady, highly intelligent, highly trained in social finesse: something which is more expertly deployed in the USA than in, say, Paris or London, because more is usually at stake. And by more, in this context, I mean money. It must be reassuring to have snobbism based on such a solid foundation, not on the

86

ever-shifting morass which represents social values in Europe — where they exist. European snobbism is a fantasm; American snobbism is Mrs Schuyler Hartog, wearing the Schuyler diamonds and sitting in her box at the Hartog Center of the Performing Arts on opening night. You know where you are. I have a sneaking suspicion that Constance Sherwood King knew exactly where she was as soon as she heard the name Ruth Shallon. I don't for one moment think she really needed to consult her file, but did so — opening a beautiful Louis Quinze armoire and poring over a fat folder — in order to get her thoughts in order and her answers prepared.

"Oh yes," she said, turning back to us. "She was a lovely girl, not at all a bad actress. I see here that one of my colleagues wrote, ' . . . a beautiful performance. Playing a bad woman is easy for any actress, but playing a good one is a great test. Miss Shallon makes Alison's virtue and her goodness of heart shine out into the auditorium like the beam of a lighthouse.' Nice. I remember the play. Trite, but she stole the show."

It was touching to see Marisa's natural pleasure on hearing this praise. She said, "Is there anything about the movie Dad made up here around . . . around that time? I think it was about pioneers and the Oregon Trail."

Connie replaced the file and rejoined us. "As a matter of fact I remember it quite well — one of the first to use us as a location. Well, there may have been a few Westerns. It was called The Wagon Rests, and it wasn't very good."

"I think Mother was in it."

"Possibly." She spread fine, long-fingered hands and added, "When it comes to identifying any friends she may have had in the theater I'm afraid I can't help you. And of course the old Playhouse was pulled down years ago, more's the pity, it was just the right size."

Her grey eyes had rested on me: a somewhat quizzical look, or was I imagining it? She added, "I could call the critic I quoted just now, my ex-colleague in my ex-job. He's getting up there in years, but he might be able to think of a few names."

I don't know what Marisa was about to answer, but I forestalled her. She probably couldn't see the writing on the wall, it was plain to me: another name for it would be 'ladylike passing of the buck'. I said, "No, Connie, don't bother. There are some other leads Marisa can try." And to my not-niece: "You have an address in Beaverton, don't you?"

"Yes." One of the names she'd taken from her mother's Christmas-card list. She was looking a trifle bewildered, and my heart went out to her. I remembered, from my own adolescence, how bewildering adult changes of direction could seem: sudden and arbitrary.

I said, "Thank you anyway, Connie.

I hope we haven't made you late for luncheon." She smiled at my purposely stagey production of the word. I think this is why we get on so well together, we share the same sense of humor and we play the same games. But she definitely, oh definitely, was not about to play Marisa's game.

We said correct goodbyes, and indeed were halfway down the marble steps leading from front door to drive when Connie reappeared at the top of them. "Will, I nearly forgot. I found that reference you wanted for your book."

She crooked a finger at me and I went back up the steps. In the hall, a properly subfusc Edwardian entrance hall complete with Art-Deco stained-glass windows, she said, "I think you'd better stop that girl asking questions, my dear."

How much did she know? Not everything, I thought, but certainly something. I saw through the still-open door Marisa and Nick locked in what appeared to be argument: unusual. I said to Connie, "It seemed rather a nice idea, the surprise birthday party." We looked at one another in silence, adjusting to the rules of this particular game.

She nodded. "Me, I'm not crazy about surprises."

"Me neither."

"Then I expect we understand each other, we usually do."

Marisa turned towards my car. Nick caught her arm and turned her back to face him. Connie said, "Stop her asking questions. Why not send her home?"

"Easier said than done with modern kids." I wasn't sure I was about to do the right thing, but I knew I'd learn a lot from her reaction: "Does the name Hartman come into this?"

She gave me a hard look, harder than anything I'd imagined to be in her repertoire, and she didn't answer the question. She said, "Will, she's walking along the edge of a precipice and she

2

Ruth

1

WHEN I walked down the steps of the Sherwood King mansion for the second time that day I was deep in thought, as Connie had intended. Her mode was always so elliptical that you were never quite sure exactly what she'd been implying — the actual words often having little to do with it. I had a sneaking suspicion that she knew the whole story. My mention of Hartman had elicited what was, for her, an outspoken warning: Marisa was on the edge of a dangerous precipice and, if she went on asking questions, there were people who might push her over. In an oblique way this seemed to corroborate her far from friendly reception at the Hartman offices, caused by a mere mention of the man's name.

Of course it was a nice idea that I ought to send her home and thereby shut her up; the only problem being that in reality there wasn't the faintest hope of doing any such thing; she was determined to find her real father, come hell or high water, and unfortunately she was convinced his name was Hartman. There were two consolations: the man was quite evidently difficult to trace; and as soon as I talked to her mother, at any moment now, Ruth was going to appear in Oregon forthwith. She held the truth in all its detail, and would know exactly how to deal with this awkward triangular problem — mother, daughter, lover. After all, it was her own very private concern.

My responsibility, as I saw it, was to remember Connie's warning, so that if danger reared its head I'd be ready to force, coax or trick the girl into taking evasive action. In the meantime I didn't intend to mention it; the search might not lead anywhere near her precipice. The trouble with this kind of decision is that you can't always tell when an apparently harmless situation has suddenly turned dangerous. The level of radiation can become critical without anybody noticing.

Nick and Marisa, who had stopped arguing, both turned beautifully innocent faces towards me. Marisa said, "A lot of help *she* was!"

I said, "Yes and no."

"What does that mean?"

"Exactly what it says — she was and she wasn't a help. If a woman like that decides not to give information it's almost as helpful as when she actually gives it." This was true with or without the lady's warning. Marisa thought about it and then added it to her growing lexicon of adult behavior. I added, "Now I'm calling your mother like I said I would."

"But, Will, even if she drops everything — "

"And I think she will."

"Even then, it'll be hours before she gets here."

"Suits me. Better than having to drive up from Astoria all over again."

Nick said, "And you don't want us around."

"Correct."

"So we could go back to your pad."

"Sure." I was wondering what their argument had been about; it seemed to be well and truly over now. Marisa took his arm and said, "Why don't we take in a movie?"

"OK."

I said, "Look, I'll give you a nice lunch and then you can take in your movie, how's that?"

"Great. Will there be seafood?"

"Excellent seafood."

As soon as we got to Jake's, in downtown Portland, I left them poring over the menu and went to make my call in the bar — from which their tender years excluded them. This time, Ruth answered so quickly that she must have been sitting with the phone at her elbow. So my earlier reasoning had probably been correct: no tennis. I'd better watch that Marisa, she could sneak up on you. I said, "Ruth, I called around 9.30. Luanne said you were out."

"Will! Oh my God, is she up there?"

"Arrived last night."

"Luanne's a fool. I was only in the garden. Why didn't you call right away? We've been demented."

"Guess."

"Yes, of course. I'm sorry. We . . . We thought she'd gone to Santa Fe."

"That's what you were meant to think."

"She didn't drive up alone?"

"No, Nick's with her."

"I wonder if he's contacted *his* parents. I'll call anyway, his mother's a dear. Will — is she OK?"

"At the moment. But I'm told she

may not stay OK if she asks too many questions."

Silence. I said, "Ruth?"

"Sorry. I was thinking."

"Going to tell me what it means?"

"Yes. No, not on the phone. I'll come up right away. Will, who flies there these days?"

"Several airlines. From Burbank."

"Burbank's easy. I can hear you're not at home. Where are you?"

"Restaurant in Portland." I gave her the number. "We haven't ordered yet."

"I'll get back to you as soon as I've booked a flight. Fifteen, twenty minutes."

"Fine."

"And Will . . . can you stop her asking questions?"

"I don't think so. Maybe you can."

"Please try. Whoever told you that . . . was probably right." She sounded exhausted, and the exhausting part hadn't even begun.

When she called back twenty-five minutes later I didn't take it at the table but again went to the bar. I felt it was better if mother and daughter didn't talk until they were face to face; even then there'd probably be more than enough misunderstandings. Ruth may have agreed; she didn't ask to speak to Marisa. Her Alaska flight arrived at 5.15. I told her I'd meet it.

During the course of an enormous and expensive lunch I learned a little more, not much, about this young odd couple. "I don't know why she likes me," he said. "Dozens of guys chase after her; I guess I'm a rest."

"I like you," replied Marisa, with absolute truth I'm sure, "because you're you."

"Suits me just fine; I dig being envied. I guess I'm the most envied guy around. And when it kind of slipped out we'd shared a bed after this party . . . Wow!"

Marisa said, "His folks are punchy. I mean they were pretty damn sure he was gay, and then he takes up with me."

"Dad's a redneck," added Nick cheerfully. "Automobile mechanic. Loves two things, his job and football — oh, and my mom I guess. Sits down in front of the TV with a six-pack and a bag of popcorn, know the type?"

What made these two so charming was the obvious fact that they came from such vastly different backgrounds. They restored my confidence in the American Way, which had taken some pretty hard knocks this time around. I realized later, wise after the event, that Marisa had still not referred to Hartman. On the other hand I did notice she was holding her soapstone toad in her right hand. I'm afraid I failed to draw conclusions from either of these facts. I merely went to the bar and treated myself to a really good cognac. Then I walked up to Powell's, that great bookstore where, as far as I'm concerned, two hours can pass in twenty minutes; and did. With the result that I got trapped in the late-afternoon crawl (why is it called a rush hour?) and only just made the airport in time.

★ ★ ★

What an elegant and truly beautiful woman she is, my brother's wife. She takes me by surprise every time I see her, whether the interim has been long or short. She looked as weary as her voice had sounded, but that kind of beauty can take weariness in its stride. As we hugged she said, "Was I snappish on the phone? I'm sorry."

"And I'm sorry I couldn't call you earlier, she'd probably have taken off."

"Yes. I wasn't thinking straight. You can imagine how it's been down there. Jack sends his love by the way. He wanted to come up with me."

"I thought he was in preproduction."

"He is. He couldn't possibly leave at this stage — they can't find a woman to play opposite Railton."

"Suicide."

"And he knew it. But he's beside

101

himself with anxiety."

"We'll call him this evening."

When we were in the car she said, "Will, who gave you that warning about questions being dangerous?"

"Connie Sherwood King. Know her?"

"Only by name."

A glance at her face told me how desperately anxious she really was, and how uncertain. I knew that the truth wouldn't help her much at this moment, but withholding it could achieve nothing and might even cause harm. I said, "Ruth, you'd better know right away — Marisa thinks her real father is called Hartman."

Her head jerked around; she stared at me, shocked green eyes wide. I continued, "And it was that name which made Connie warn me."

When she could find her voice she said, "How the hell did she find out?"

"You mean she's right?"

"Yes."

"Your old colleague, Julie Wrenn, told her."

"Julie! I haven't seen her in years."

"Your daughter's a crafty little girl, Ruth."

"But . . . Julie didn't even know him."

"A unit on location gossips like a bunch of old women."

"Yes." She rubbed a finger over her eyelids. "Come to think of it she did see us together — once, at a restaurant. But she *couldn't* have known he was Marisa's father, nobody knew."

"She didn't say he was — just a boyfriend. Marisa took a shot in the dark. As soon as she got to Portland she tried to find him."

"Oh God!"

"And failed."

"He won't be easy to find, I'm sure of that." And, with a glance: "Will, I'm sorry she involved you in all this."

"Oh come on — haven't you and Jack ever put yourselves out for me? God knows how I can help, but if I can . . ."

I certainly couldn't help with the

situation which faced us when we reached my apartment: Marisa and Nick had disappeared with all their belongings; they had even made up the spare bed for Mother. A note on my desk said, "Many thanks. See you later. Love to Mom." Only now did I recall that on parting from me in Jake's she'd been holding Cross-eye: "I always take him if I'm going to do something way-out." Ruth had come all this way to confront a daughter who declined to be confronted. "Oh God," she said, "why?"

"Ruth, she's dead set on finding this guy, and she thinks you're dead set on stopping her."

"I'm not. I just have to find him first, before she does. Where do you suppose they've gone?"

"Motel. And don't say it — there are hundreds of motels around here, vacation land, remember?"

She managed a shaky smile. "Dear Will. How come you're so like Jack, yet so utterly different?"

"Talking of Jack, you were going to call him."

"And tell him what?"

I suppose honest people really do find it difficult to lie. I'm a writer, lies are my stock in trade. "Tell him the kids have gone for a hamburger, and I'm taking you out to dinner."

"He'll want Marisa to call as soon as she gets back."

Yes, that was exactly what he'd want; so perhaps the truth was better. "Tell him she's in hiding because she's afraid you'll stop her finding this guy." She thought about it; then nodded. I pointed to the open door of my bedroom. "Talk in there, it'll be easier."

When she emerged after fifteen minutes she looked more exhausted than ever; like all high-powered, get-up-and-go people, Jack can draw the energy right out of you. I asked how he was. "Not great. He thinks I'm holding out on him. I guess I am — kind of."

"What you need is a really good drink."

"That's exactly what I need."

"OK. On one condition . . ."

She laughed. "My God, it's about *time* I told you."

2

Once or twice a year the old Playhouse Theater in Portland would present a piece by Shakespeare. Ruth Shallon had made a stab at Hermione, wronged heroine of the poet's late play, *A Winter's Tale*. She says she wasn't very good, but her performance had been found deeply touching — not a dry eye in the house. I expect she brought to it the kind of radiant innocence which had so impressed the critic whom Connie had quoted.

A Winter's Tale had been chosen for one of those charity galas so favored by Americans, and prominent on the committee, as on many another, were Mr and Mrs Scott Hartman, pillars of the establishment, possibly the richest people in the Northwest: 'old money'. At a reception after the performance Scott Hartman met Ruth Shallon. Mutual attraction was instant.

How difficult it is to describe the emotions which fling people headlong into a love affair. Do you accept their view of events, always distorted by those very emotions, or do you strain that view through the sieve of your own emotional experience, removing a lot of unnecessary bits and pieces in the process, but perhaps ending up with only a watery version of the truth? Seventeen years later, even Ruth herself can't say, "Love at first sight, I guess," without an edge of derision sharpening her voice. The old witch Dame Nature is at work, casting her spell and not caring in the least that it blinds you and makes a fool of you — not caring either that once the spell has worn off you'll scarcely be able to believe it ever existed; her intention will have been accomplished for the nth time, a child (like Marisa) will probably have been produced, thus perpetuating the species. Marriage? Dame Nature has never heard of it. Con of all cons, many will say, and there's hardly a human being who isn't at some time the patsy.

So, in the knowledge that we all know how much or how little it means, let's use Ruth's own term: love at first sight. Since love is a tender and slow-growing plant, again as we all know, what we probably mean is 'sex at first sight', and that's what it usually is. Ruth Shallon, actress, and Scott Hartman, multi-millionaire, fell in love, and soon, because he was a handsome and virile man of forty-four and she was a beautiful and healthy girl of twenty-four, they also fell into bed. My sister-in-law could not for the life of her keep self-mockery out of her description of all this: "Will, honest to God it's such a corny story — actress and millionaire — diamonds are a girl's best friend — but I was . . . I mean, I don't even remember it too clearly but I was madly in love with him, I must have been. And he was in love with me. What the hell else is there to say?"

Absolutely nothing, she's right: from that point of view. From other points of view there's a lot to say, because Scott Hartman was married to a woman he'd grown to dislike intensely, and between them they'd produced a daughter and a much-loved son who had died, aged thirteen, not too long before he met Ruth. The year of this love affair was 1978. Hartman had married Christina Allborn in 1963. The son, Tom, had been born in 1964 and Susan in 1966. I'll take Ruth's word for it that wealth had not spoiled her lover by the time she met him. Personally I think inherited wealth spoils anyone it touches; Christina, who came of a 'good' but poor family, and Susan her daughter, and Mark Lindsey her son-in-law are three prime examples.

The Hartman money came from a number of typically Northwestern sources, originally from shipping. Great-grandfather Hartman had been quick to realize that Oregon's timber needed to be transported to the various timberless lands prepared to pay large sums of money for it, Japan to the fore; so while he was about it why not lease or buy land, and then transport his own timber, thereby making what could be called a clear profit. As the territory opened up, with all its bounteous natural wealth, he found himself transporting people too: up and down the great Columbia, and then by means of the railroad, of which he also bought chunks, across the continent. To build the railroads many slaves were required: Chinese slaves who also needed to be transported in order to create the lines of transportation; and more Chinese to work the new canning industry at the end of the line, also in part owned by Hartman. And of course there was a tidy sum to be made from the millions of oysters, most of them from what is now Washington

State, and most of those from Willapa Bay; when these were transported to gold-struck San Francisco they found buyers who were willing to pay almost anything, sometimes in gold dust, for a good fresh dozen.

At Great-grandfather's death, all his descendants really had to do was sit back and watch the fortune multiplying itself. Of course they couldn't avoid making more money, mainly out of timber and fishing and transportation, but their prime concern was to tend the money garden, opening a few banks, investing in whatever took their fancy, like oil, educating their progeny to be worthy of all this wealth, and generally poking their fingers into every pie from politics to, it was said, prostitution. The standard American story, and a wondrous story it is.

But the story has to be continued into the next generation, and the next. It stands to reason that if Grandfather possesses only a fraction of the character of his own father, and if inherited money is a softening factor, then Grandfather will be a lesser man, and his son lesser still. By the time this diminuendo of worth reached the present day, wealth and laziness had obviously riddled the House of Hartman like woodworm. I've no doubt that Scott, when Ruth met him, was an attractive and charming man, but he could no more escape the downward spiral than a river can escape from flowing downhill.

By the time he'd been married three years, often a time when men pause and take stock, his wife Christina considered that she'd performed her duties, both to the Hartman dynasty and to members of her own family who would never want for anything again. She was one of those black-haired magnolia-skinned beauties who are often assumed to be bundles of passion; Christina was passionless; she was also cold and calculating and as tough as an old boot. When her husband fell out of love and came to his senses, he was probably appalled to discover what he'd brought into his house. He began to retreat from her in a series of untidy rearguard actions. He was only thirty-two, full of life and money, and his relationships with various other women kept the gossips happy for years.

Christina knew, and probably told him, that her own position was secure for life, and if he wanted to have squalid little love affairs it was entirely his own business; she intended to ignore them. Occasionally she gratified her body with this or that man; emotion was never involved, naturally, but she probably needed to bolster her ego from time to time, proving to herself that she was still beautiful and desirable. Many couples, and not always wealthy ones, jog along in loveless parodies of marriage, and the Hartmans might have continued to do so into old age, had it not been for two abrupt alterations in the pattern. The first occurred when their son Thomas, aged thirteen, went sailing on the Columbia with his Uncle Matt,

Scott's only brother. They were caught in a sudden devastating squall which came howling out of the east, from the snowy highlands around Mount Hood. Both of them were drowned, which meant that Scott Hartman was now sole heir to the vast fortune, also that his own heir no longer existed.

Christina Hartman took this dispensation of Providence as a personal affront, a slap in the face. She was thirty-eight years old at the time, painstakingly preserved to look a good ten years younger. Women, particularly rich ones, don't really want to start having children again at that age but, all things (like the Hartman name and wealth) considered, she was willing to go through with it. Her husband was not willing to go through with it, another slap in the face, and may have said, after a couple of drinks, that he had no intention of going to bed with her ever again; he may even have added — legend asserts he did — that it was like going to bed with a dish of half-melted ice cream. As for heirs, let the daughter have it. One can't exactly hear his great-grandfather making a remark like this. Christina was wounded to the core of her spoiled, rich, American womanhood: and that's some core.

The second alteration in life's pattern occurred a little over a year later. Nobody knows how she first heard of her husband's entanglement with an attractive young actress — no doubt she had plenty of 'friends' who couldn't wait to tell her. She was probably not in the least worried, it had all happened before; but when it became evident, with the passing of time, that he was deeply in love with the girl . . . This had never happened before and must not be allowed to continue now. The alimony, of course, would be enormous, but a mere scatter cushion compared to the giant bolster upon which she now reclined.

She didn't have many allies to

support the attack on a family level. Scott's father was dead, and his feckless mother preferred queering it alone in Rome to sharing the Oregon throne which she'd occupied for twenty-five years before her son's marriage; she didn't like her daughter-in-law anyway. Brother Matthew had died at the same time as the only son, and though there were various cousins and an aunt or two, they'd be no help now because Christina had antagonized them all years ago.

Another factor, which she had never taken into account before, complicated the issue; she'd known that Scott loved their son, but being constitutionally incapable of love herself she had no idea how deep that love went, nor how bitterly he mourned the boy's death. Ruth, a kind-hearted and natural girl, understood both emotions completely; indeed it was part of the 'cliché' of their love affair that he was the standard rich middle-aged man with a tragic past: his marriage was a farce and he had recently lost the only part of it he truly valued.

It was around now that he told her the other, older thing he held against his wife. Long before, when he was a very young man, at around the time he'd first met Christina, and ignored her, he'd been in love with a beautiful girl who came from his kind of family; as far as Ruth could make out she was one of those delicately fair creatures who are at their best wearing chiffon by moonlight, and who always arouse men's protective instincts. In any case, it was first love, romantic and sweet and forever. It had been going on for three or four months, with talk of an engagement, when suddenly the girl withdrew; was never in when he called; had even gone on a trip to Europe with her mother. A frantic young Scott searched for her in vain, and searched, as vainly, to find some reason for her behavior.

He found none. The romance faded and died, and the young man, bleeding from aborted first love, wouldn't have minded dying with it. Christina, black and white and dazzling (and poor), came at him on the rebound. Only later, years later, did he discover that she'd known the girl quite well and had poured little drops of poison into the shell-like ear. That Scott Hartman, so good-looking but his private life . . . ! The poison never changes and never fails to work; always hints at married women and prostitutes, wild parties and possibly, my dear, drugs! Needless to say this story only made Ruth Shallon love him all the more, if such a thing were possible.

I'd found myself wondering what Ruth's mother, Corinne, had thought of her daughter's love affair; it could never in a hundred years have been hidden from her, she has a nose for secrets. But apparently Corinne had been widowed two years earlier and, exhausted by months of nursing a sick husband, Oregon born, had gone back to the only city in the world, New

York, on an extended visit to various relatives.

★ ★ ★

My sister-in-law had broken off periodically during the telling of her story: every time a car slowed down outside, every time a door closed somewhere in the big house. As gently as possible I said, "Ruth, my dear, it's no good expecting her to turn up now, she won't. She daren't."

"But she can't begin to find Scott on her own. I have all the clues and she has none, and I'm not too sure I can find him."

"Do you have to?"

"Yes, I do."

"Before she does, I think you said."

She nodded. I didn't at that moment ask the obvious question; slowly and painfully, as we get older, we sometimes learn that there's a correct time for every question, and if you don't wait for it you're liable not to get any answer at all. I said, "Powder your nose, or whatever, and I'll take you out to eat." Wryly I thought that just at a time when I'd congratulated myself on being too busy with my writing to spend much money, temporarily in short supply, I found I was having to assuage the appetites of the Adams family who were used to good restaurants and good food. Since there are no first-rate restaurants in Astoria I took her across the famous four-mile-long bridge to the Shelburne in Washington State.

Over oysters, from that same Willapa Bay which had added a little something to her lover's family fortune, she told me about the assault Christina Hartman had mounted against her husband and his actress girlfriend. It had been savage and remorseless, and must be said to have achieved its purpose in that the relationship was finally destroyed and Ruth sent packing, just as another girl had been sent packing many years before. But the wife may have found it a somewhat hollow victory when she discovered that her husband's former indifference had now turned to spiteful hostility. He refused to enter the family home, didn't speak to her if they met in public, and said some pretty nasty, but true, things about her behind her back; he also cut her allowance to a minimum.

This last wouldn't have worried her overmuch because in fifteen years of marriage she had managed to salt away a considerable fortune of her own, not to mention a second fortune in jewelry. On top of this he threatened to divorce her if she refused to divorce him: he had evidence of her most recent passionless liaison. The fact that the family lawyers all considered divorce to be out of the question, in spite of the huge fees attorneys always milk from such litigation, proves how profitable they must have found the status quo. The head attorney, Wesley Ryder (still very much around, as we were to discover), finally made Scott Hartman listen: divorce would create more problems than it would solve, and with his kind of money what did divorce matter anyway? He need never speak to Christina again as long as he lived. Of course Ryder had one eye on the daughter, Susan, next of kin, heir to the whole shebang, a golden goose for the future. In the end, with Ruth gone, Hartman said, "What the hell!" and simply disappeared.

Over profiteroles, I asked her, "If he'd settled for divorce, would he have married you?"

More than seventeen years later she could only shrug. "He said he would. Men are weird. He seemed so strong, but underneath . . ."

"I told you — inherited money does that to them."

"Could be. I know Jack's just the opposite. He's so gentle, a lot of people think he's weak. And then, suddenly . . ." She ended on a gesture.

"They find themselves kneecapped." Naturally. How could he have made it in the Hollywood jungle if he hadn't been tough beneath the charm?

"Scott talked a lot and threw his weight around, and made everyone, even Wesley Ryder, very nervous. But . . . I don't think he'd have gone through with marrying me."

"But the relationship was wrecked."

"Yes. I've often wondered if that proves it wasn't . . . wasn't a Grade A relationship in the first place."

"I don't see why it should — with Christina Hartman out to kill it stone dead."

"And if it had been really strong, would I . . . could I have married Jack so soon afterwards?"

"Self-preservation. It can beat love to a pulp any day."

"I guess."

"And haven't you noticed — mothers will undertake almost anything on behalf of their tiny ones?"

"I've noticed." A wry smile. "Was marrying Jack that kind of undertaking? Am I such a calculating bitch?"

"Oh come on, Ruth. Thank God women *do* calculate, it's what makes them women. If the average man can't size up a problem in sixty seconds he either shoots it or goes out and gets drunk."

At least this made her smile; she was beginning to shed that painful tension.

"And I don't suppose you were 'in love' with Jack the way you'd been 'in love' with Scott Hartman. That was gorgeous old sex, pure and simple, and if you want my opinion, which you don't, it wouldn't have lasted anyway. But you and Jack have stayed together a long, long time — isn't that what they call love?"

"I think so. I hope so."

"When did he come bouncing onto the stage dressed as Sir Galahad?"

"After I'd been with Scott about . . . five months."

"Five months — I bet you never even noticed him."

"Not much."

"But he fell for you right away."

"No, I don't think so."

"He thinks so. We have our moments of intimacy, you know."

"They're not very noticeable."

"Late at night, over a bottle." To me the amazing thing has always been that my impatient and precipitate brother managed to play the waiting game without blowing his top. "He must have wanted you very much. Well he did, he told me that too. The only woman for him, and he knew it immediately."

"Will . . . I shall cry in a minute."

"Cry on, probably do you good. Anyway, it all stands out a mile, that's why the rest of us get jealous from time to time. What happened, Ruth — between takes three and four while the wagon was resting out there by the Willamette?"

"I loved working with him. I loved it all anyway, the camaraderie and the awful jokes, it was all so *young*."

"And so were you — twenty-four.

125

And Scott was forty-four."

"Oh God! Can it have been that . . . brutal?"

"Yes."

"You don't know how his wife poisoned everything for us. I felt . . . hounded, dirty. I couldn't face going out with him any more, and we'd always had such fun going out together. Not to his places, grand places, but to all kinds of funny . . . You know, you've been in love."

I knew exactly.

"Suddenly there were photographers around every corner, and snide little bits in the paper, and . . . She meant to turn it all sour and she succeeded. Towards the end we were both unhappy most of the time."

Yes, I could see it all very plainly: the beautiful girl trying to keep things the way they'd once been, and the rich spoiled man festering in his own anger, his own selfishness; the souffle so often subsides as soon as it's taken out of the oven. But over there, in that other life, it was all satisfying hard work in front of the camera, and laughs after the 'cut', and the terrible jokes for which movie crews are famous, and the director's adoring eyes — he was twenty-nine. It was all young.

"Then," she said, "Julie Wrenn said I ought to go down to LA and give it a whirl, I might have a great future. And I . . . OK, I cut and ran."

I thought about this; then said, "I'm not sure why Connie Sherwood King thought Marisa's questions might be dangerous. Unless . . . "

"Unless what?"

"Unless Connie knew you were carrying Scott Hartman's child."

"I told you, Will, nobody knew. I didn't even tell my mother." She leaned across the table, emphasizing her point: "Scott and his wife never got together again after me, I was the big break. Christina went around saying I'd wrecked their marriage."

"Which had been wrecked for years."

"Ten or more, and everyone knew it."

"Including Connie?"

"Obviously. Why else would she want you to stop Marisa asking questions? Not because she's Scott's child, nobody knows about that, but because she's *my* child — the scarlet woman's child digging up all the old dirt."

She was right: it would have brought Christina out of her corner punching. And if she was the kind of woman I imagined her to be she wouldn't for one moment doubt that the girl was acting maliciously, probably prompted by Ruth. It would have been a dangerous situation all right, and Connie had known it; and had declined to give us any information for that reason. A wise lady and a good friend.

I said, "Sorry. I interrupted. You cut and ran — with my brother close behind."

"Not very close. Or maybe I just didn't know it then. When we first got to LA he took me out to dinner a few times, he was obviously interested . . . "

"But you were still brooding over Scott."

"Yes. Though in a way it was . . . This is going to sound awful. It was a relief to have . . . escaped."

"Sounds perfectly natural to me."

"I felt I could breathe again. As far as Jack was concerned, it wasn't really until he followed me down to Santa Fe . . . "

"Ah, the New Mexico connection. Marisa didn't explain it."

"You were right," said Ruth, sipping coffee, "my child is crafty. I think she must get it from Corinne — like the eyes. She left a map of New Mexico in her bedroom."

"What did that mean?"

"It was a red herring. We thought she'd gone chasing off in the wrong direction. She was born there, why shouldn't her real father live there?"

"A smart red herring."

"Yes. And of course Julie must have

told her we made another movie together down that way."

"She did. What happened in Santa Fe — when Jack followed you there?"

"That was the showdown. He cornered me and I had to tell him I was pregnant."

"And he said he didn't give a damn."

"That's exactly what he said. My God, Will, probably not one man in a hundred would have said that."

"A rare bird, my brother."

"We made a plan. When the location was over I'd stay on. I was beginning to show by then. God knows why the whole crew wasn't onto it — but they weren't, not even Julie. So I stayed, and Corinne came down from New York and joined me. She absolutely loathed New Mexico. And Jack came down whenever he could make it. We were married there, and five months later Marisa was born."

"A little New Mexican."

"Jack bought our first Hollywood house while I was away. We only had a few friends then — he told them I was having the baby in Santa Fe to be with my mother."

"No lie anyway."

"And a few months later back I came with a rather elderly infant, but if anyone noticed they didn't say."

★ ★ ★

Astoria looks beautiful on a clear night from the Washington side of the river; looks large and important too, with all those lights climbing the hill and tumbling along the Columbia from Young's Bay in the west to Tongue Point in the east.

For a while we drove in silence. Recalling all she'd told me, I said, "There's one thing I don't quite understand. Why did Scott Hartman allow you to go before he'd even played his trump card?"

"Trump card?"

"Yes, of course — the fact that you were pregnant with his child. Christina couldn't have topped it, he'd have floored her."

"He couldn't play that card, Will. I told you, nobody knew."

It took me a moment to assimilate this; and then I was the one who was floored. "Not . . . Ruth, not even your lover?"

"Not even Scott."

It doesn't matter how much you may think you know about the hidden depths of women and their particular reasoning which men only imagine they can understand, they can still surprise you every time.

So there it was, the answer to the question which, in my apartment, I'd thought better of asking: why did she feel she had to get to Hartman before her daughter, their daughter? Because he didn't even know Marisa existed.

3

Scott

1

AT eight o'clock next morning, Marisa and Nick — who had indeed spent the night in a motel, after a takeaway meal of pizza and beer and ice cream consumed in their room — were waiting in her Subaru station wagon at the end of my street. The first part of their plan had been systematically worked out; waiting was a bore but an integral component, ameliorated somewhat by coffee and donuts.

All unknowing, Ruth and I sat in the bay window eating our own breakfast. The keeper of my boat may have been right about an indian summer but it hadn't arrived yet. The sun was shining brilliantly and a cold north wind was ruffling the Columbia into angry little wavelets; the ocean's incoming tide and the river's outgoing flow were fighting their usual twice-daily battle and had reached deadlock: the kind of water I choose if I want to take *Mary Celeste II* over to the Washington shore. A tanker, ugly — but nothing can look really ugly on such a pristine day — was nosing her way upstream.

"So," I asked, "what's the plan?"

My sister-in-law was a different woman this morning; a good night's sleep had worked its usual wonders. Her reply was oblique: "I didn't tell you — Scott was very sick, about nine years ago. Automobile accident. He was quite badly smashed up. Drunk."

"Figures."

The jade eyes searched my face. "You have nothing but contempt for him."

"Some pity."

"He is . . . was admirable in many ways."

134

"What does his accident have to do with trying to find him?"

"Maybe a lot. I'm going to talk to his wife."

This really took me by surprise. "I'd have thought she was the last person you'd want to talk to."

"I think he went back home — after all the operations. So how can I see him without seeing her too?"

"I don't believe he'd ever have gone back."

"Seventeen years is a long time, Will. They're neither of them young any more, they must . . . have come to terms; it's the only decent option."

"I think you're judging them by your own high standards. How do you know about all this anyway — the car crash and so on?"

"I have a good friend in Beaverton who used to write and send me clippings. I asked her to stop. I had another life to lead, and I didn't want the old life interfering with it."

"So you're going to march right in

and ask Christina if you can see your lover."

She grimaced. "Put like that it sounds pretty scary."

"It'll be more than scary if someone connects you with Marisa's little exploit at Hartman."

"Why should they? I'm not going to the office anyway, I'm going to his home. And you always talk as if Marisa and I were alike."

"You are."

"Only to people who know us well. Most people see no resemblance at all."

This was true, but I still thought it a crazy thing to do. I said, "He won't be there, and you'll have stuck your neck out for nothing."

She turned to me: a cool, calm, faintly amused stare. I said, "Oh my God, you *want* to face her!"

"Since it's probably the quickest way of finding him . . . " "No, no — you want it. Don't pretend you don't know what I mean."

She looked out over the water to the hills of Washington State. "I'm quite prepared to face her if it serves a purpose, yes. If it served no purpose I wouldn't go near her."

I didn't believe it. Women have their own codes of behavior, based on their own philosophy, their own morality — hadn't she given me extraordinary proof of it last night? I couldn't rationalize her decision not to tell the man she was pregnant, and I couldn't rationalize her willingness, now, to face his bitch-wife. But an hour later, when she came out of the bedroom dressed for the encounter, I knew I'd at least been right about her wanting to do it. She looked stunning — she has perfect dress sense. Smiling, she said, "And I'm not wearing a thing she can't label with the maker's name. And price. I've met quite a few women like that since she sent me packing. You play them at their own game."

"Rather a waste of finery if you can't get in."

"I'll get in." She took a slip of paper from her purse and went to the phone. After a few moments a voice answered, and for a change not a recorded voice: Ruth said, "Yes, I know it's the old number. Mrs Hartman gave me her new one and like a fool I left it in California."

Having gone closer, I could hear the voice replying that the Hartman number wasn't listed and couldn't be given to anyone. Ruth said, "I'm not asking you to give it me. Surely you can just connect me, it's an urgent matter."

The voice said something about a supervisor, and there was a lengthy silence, followed by, "Your name please?"

"Ruth . . . Shallon."

"One moment please."

Ruth extended the receiver to my ear. I could hear a faint ringing tone — then someone answering it — then indistinct conversation. Finally, "I'm connecting you."

"Good morning. This is Mrs Hartman's secretary."

"Is Mrs Hartman available this morning? I'd like to see her. Only for a short while."

"I'll ask. Was the name Shallon, Ruth Shallon?"

"Yes." The fuse had been lit. The ensuing detonation may have been muffled — I failed to hear it; only, after quite a long pause, "Mrs Hartman could give you a half-hour at noon, Miss Shallon."

"I'll be there." She replaced the phone and looked at me, deep in thought. "We'll be there. I'll need moral support — and I think a suit will help."

"Ruth, I came to Oregon to escape suits."

"Your writer's curiosity will look better in a suit."

I really needed no persuading. Privately, I thought that a suit was a small price to pay for a meeting with Christina Hartman.

So we set off for Portland, watched with lip-smacking curiosity by Mrs Swensen, of all people; I didn't know she ever moved from her chair. I could hear the comment: "A different woman every night, Andy, how about that?"

The journey was quiet until we once again hit Interstate 5, which was playing its role to the hilt that morning; the left lane was closed and we processed at an orderly rubbernecking speed, passing what must have been at least a ten-car pile-up, all sirens and flashing, blinding lights: nothing if you go by comparisons, which I don't. Ten-car, eighty-car, it's still death and destruction, and more lives destined to be spent in wheelchairs. Yet as soon as we repossessed our left lane, off they all went: seventy, eighty, even ninety miles an hour, speed limit sixty-five. Why, you may ask, *sell* cars capable of a hundred and twenty miles per hour and over? Answer: because people just love the idea of speed and will pay for it. Better than loving heroin or alcohol,

I suppose, but no less deadly. We're all lemmings.

Portland is full of hills. EastWest Drive is exactly what its name implies, at least at the higher, grander end. Expensive houses, standing in an acre or two and facing west, are gradually superseded by mansions standing in ten, twenty, thirty acres, the last few on top of the hill commanding the famous view both to east and west: from Mount Hood, when visible, ruling the Cascade Range to little Saddle Mountain, rarely visible, highest point of the Coast Range. Number Seven was a sprawling nineteenth-century Italianate confection sporting an elegant tower, or should one say 'campanile'? At one time it apparently contained twenty-two bedrooms: before many of them were turned into saunas, exercise rooms, spacious staff apartments — I almost envied the staff.

The Italianate lodge, which would have satisfied most people as a private residence, was an impressive security blockhouse, the clasp in a chain of wall topped with jagged glass encircling, as far as one could see, the whole domain. Privacy, which means thirty urban acres of incalculable value, and safety, which means the blockhouse with its alarms and closed-circuit TV and God knows what else, are the two requisites most in demand by the very rich, or so I read. As the world disintegrates into screaming chaos they have a point.

A scrubbed and hefty young man, almost in uniform but not quite, consulted a clipboard and admitted us. The gates swung open with smooth electronic condescension. We curved through immaculately maintained lawns, past a water garden, a walled rose garden, two tennis courts, to a wide circle in front of the house: paved for silence, no nasty scrunchy gravel. There was even an imposing porte-cochere into which I did not drive. I parked well away from a Rolls, a Maserati, and a Cadillac stretch limo. My new Taurus looked poverty-stricken.

We were shown into what the secretary — attractive but conscientiously mousy, knowing her position — called the morning room. Crossing the immense marbled hall I could understand that security was perhaps necessary; there was a great deal of beautiful stuff standing around, and over the fireplace a fine Gainsborough I'd never seen before, not even in illustration: one of his pert young ladies with a lively eye, showing more ankle than her mother would have considered respectable. The morning room was cozier, but six of the smaller paintings were by Bonnard, and there was a good Manet.

About ten minutes after our arrival (those kind of people keep everyone waiting, they think it's a sign of class — it is, but not very good class), Christina Hartman made her entrance, you couldn't call it anything else, pausing in the doorway like a well-known but not very accomplished actress expecting applause. Stretching and snipping and tucking had made the 56-year-old face look a good deal younger, but there comes a stage when such adjustments overtake the adjuster and begin to have a contrary effect. Mrs Hartman had just reached that stage. The beauty, which was considerable, was on the point of turning into a beautiful mask, dead. She didn't open her mouth very wide to speak, but perhaps I'm being uncharitable, perhaps she never had.

She said, "I won't say I wasn't surprised to hear from you, I was. I agreed to see you because I was curious." During this she had assessed, as Ruth had said she would, every detail of the younger woman's appearance: clothes, jewelry (very little), shoes, purse, hairdo, and face, very much the face. She had the grace, or perhaps the effrontery, to add, "I must say you're not quite what I expected."

The contrast between them was certainly remarkable; it wasn't merely that Ruth's look was the new, soft look, whereas Christina Hartman seemed to

144

have preserved herself in a time capsule dated fifteen or even twenty years before: immaculate dark grey coat and skirt, and diamonds, which are never kind to an aging face: it was a total difference of character. Ruth's natural elegance made Mrs Hartman look haggard and oddly ostentatious.

She moved, touching Ruth's dress as she passed, with a finger which already showed signs of arthritis, that great leveler, and said, "Lucio."

"Yes."

"I can't wear him." She reached for a bell pull and jerked it once: no distant tinkle in a house that size. And no one answered, so I guessed it was a signal rather than a summons for service. Then, turning, "You're married of course."

"Yes."

"Done well for yourself, haven't you?"

This was so arrogantly condescending, grand lady to ex-kitchen maid, that I said, "Not the only one around here."

Of course it was unforgivable but the tone had enraged me. Ruth flashed me a cautionary glance. Christina Hartman turned her back on me and said, "What do you want? Why have you come back?" She made it sound as though a demand for money, perhaps with menaces, would not have surprised her.

Very evenly, her eyes daring me to intervene, Ruth replied, "I want to see Scott."

The carefully constructed face creased into unbecoming anger. "How dare you ask such a thing, you of all people, nothing but a . . . a good-time girl?"

I said, "Mrs Hartman, I'm a writer. For a small fee I'll work over your dialogue, it needs it."

She wheeled on me, dark eyes icy cold, pieces of frozen jet. "You're insolent. I don't know what you're doing here anyway."

"Neither did I until a few seconds ago. Now I realize I'm here to protect my sister-in-law from corny insults."

146

Ruth said, "Don't listen to him, I don't need protecting. As a matter of fact I was curious too — and I expected insults."

"*Why* do you want to see Scott?"

"Why not? He's an old friend. Perhaps stupidly, I thought he might be living here."

Christina Hartman wasn't very bright, but she picked up on the real meaning of 'stupidly'. I think she may have flushed — with that much make-up you can only tell by the ears and neck. "Well, you were wrong, he isn't living here."

"In that case I thought my best way of finding him would be to ask you."

"Of all the bare-faced cheek!" It wasn't just the dated vocabulary; the wretched woman had got the whole thing wrong. I hoped I wouldn't begin to feel sorry for her. Fundamentally untruthful herself, she couldn't even understand that Ruth was being straightforward. "I don't know where he is, and if I did I wouldn't tell you.

Somewhere in Europe I suppose." She should have been a consummate liar, but she wasn't even that.

Ruth said, "Then I've missed him, what a pity! Is he . . . ? Did he get over that terrible accident all right?"

"Who told you about the accident?"

"Mrs Hartman, I do have friends here, I lived here for years."

"I think you've asked enough impertinent questions. I don't know where Scott is; you'd better go."

Typically, I was beginning to feel, even this ultimatum turned out to be ill-timed. The door opened and, presumably in answer to the bell signal, a younger woman came in; she could have been no one but the daughter. If Christina Hartman had been as beautiful at the same age I wasn't surprised that Scott Hartman had desired her. Oddly enough, although she can't have been more than thirty, she gave no impression of youth, and for some reason her style in dress, hair, even manner was not unlike that of her mother. Can she have admired the prototype so much? It didn't seem possible.

"My daughter, Susan Lindsey. Mrs . . . ?"

"Adams."

"And Mr Adams, her brother-in-law."

Susan didn't acknowledge us, merely flashed us a glance of total disinterest, and said, "I've broken a nail. Isn't that *maddening*?" Her voice, the result of Vassar, I suspect, and probably an English finishing school in Switzerland, was small and precise and consciously un-American. She was as frost-bound as her mother, but in her there was no icy fire, only icy self-assurance. Watching her, it struck me that whereas Christina Hartman had needed to fight for wealth and position, this girl had been born to it and had never for one moment doubted it. Her broken nail was, at the moment and quite genuinely, the most important thing in her life.

I was just thinking how appalling it would be to be married to her, when her husband came into the room behind her. Mark Lindsey was about the only kind of man who could be married to her without finding it appalling. He was large and muscular, handsome in a coarse, even brutal, way. I could imagine Miss Vassar finding him attractive, different, animal. The correct executive suit, the obligatory tan, the sun-streaked hair didn't somehow go with the rest of him, they seemed like a disguise. His pale grey eyes were as gelid as those of his mother-in-law, who was now saying, "Mrs Adams wants to see Scott — can you imagine her daring to ask where he is? I'm quite glad we don't know."

This was the most obvious prompt I'd ever heard outside the amateur theater, which was where her performance properly belonged. Mark Lindsey now fulfilled my expectations of him by introducing a private matter which excluded Ruth completely: "Braden called. He'll come by at six if that's OK."

It was only when he spoke that I became aware of his mouth — the kind often, and mistakenly, called 'sensual' — and realized that here, without doubt, was 'Greedy-lips' who had interrogated Marisa on her ill-starred visit to the Hartman offices. Then of course it all fell into place: the reported absence of Scott Hartman himself, the executive suit, the son-in-law. I glanced at Ruth to see if she also had jumped to this conclusion — slightly raised eyebrows told me she had; and she'd been right in saying that he wouldn't connect her with Marisa in any way — he didn't.

Christina Hartman had now joined the exclusion game, with relish. "I can see Braden in the library before dinner. I have the Markhams and the Lee-Whittingstalls." They really did need someone to write the dialogue and to

151

direct it; Jack and I could have improved the production a hundredfold. Obviously Ruth shared my view. Showing a claw, far too subtle a claw for present company, she said, "We'll be going — you have so many *important* matters to discuss. I'm sorry you couldn't help me."

"I'm not," snapped Mrs Hartman. "Haven't you caused enough trouble in this family?"

"In my opinion," added her son-in-law, "you've got one hell of a nerve coming here at all."

I said, "So much for your opinion."

He glared. "What's that supposed to mean?"

"If you can't understand English I'm certainly not going to translate."

Obviously he would have liked to hit me; less obviously I wouldn't have minded hitting him back — I'm not normally a punching person. His wife may just conceivably have understood my urge (shared it?) because she looked up from filing her nail and gave me something like a sympathetic look: her only contribution to the whole exchange. Her mother decided to put me in my place: "You're a very rude young man, you should learn a little respect."

In for a dime, in for a dollar. "Actually I'm big on respect, Mrs Hartman, and I know when people don't deserve it."

Mark Lindsey jerked towards me. I noticed that he was inclined to sweat. "I think you'd better leave, and I mean right now."

"On the whole," I said, taking Ruth's arm, "that will be a pleasure."

My dear sister-in-law was genuinely angry with me, but I'm afraid I was as genuinely unrepentant. While we were getting into the car I said, "She only just stopped herself calling you a whore, and Mark Lindsey's a creep and a bully."

"No reason to antagonize them."

"Oh come on, Ruth. Let's say you knew exactly how to dress for them, and I knew exactly how to treat them. Quits."

The look she gave me betrayed the fact that although she thought my behavior ill-mannered she didn't entirely regret it. I said, "You shouldn't have taken me along; you know what the Adams boys are like, you married one." It struck me later that maybe she'd taken me along *because* she knew what the Adams boys were like: in which case she'd been expecting me to lose my temper; in which case Marisa hadn't necessarily inherited that cunning from Corinne — Corinne's daughter could well have had something to do with it. Come to that, her real reason for wanting to face Christina Hartman had been pretty suspect too, at best ambiguous.

Did I at this point consider the Hartmans a threat? I can't say I really did. The moral, if there is one, must be that you should never dismiss people's potential for evil just because they seem stupid or inept. One thing was now clear: Number Seven, EastWest Drive, was Connie's precipice; if Marisa had found the house, had inadvertently revealed her true purpose in Oregon, somebody might very possibly have pushed her over the edge.

But Scott Hartman wasn't living there, and hadn't lived there for years, and so Marisa had no need to go anywhere near the place; the search for her father would lead her in a different direction, as I'd hoped it might. Given present circumstances, this prognosis was adequate. If circumstances should change, then it might be prudent to reconsider the whole idea of a threat; for the time being, I thought, sufficient unto the day . . .

I was occupied with these thoughts as we drove out of the prison gates; but even without them I don't think I'd have noticed the Subaru station wagon parked on a side street just below the crest of the hill.

The idea had been Nick's. He had conceived it as soon as I made the deal with Marisa which opened my way to calling Ruth in LA; and he'd suggested it while I was having that last-minute conversation with Connie Sherwood King in her Art-Deco hall. Marisa disagreed right away, she wanted action and she wanted it at once; hence the mysterious argument I'd witnessed between them. But beginning then and continuing later, after their hearty meal at Jake's, he had made her see that no amount of rushing to and fro, no amount of what she called action, would achieve half as much as the waiting game and a little patience. "You don't think your mom's coming up here just to stop you finding this guy."

"That's exactly what she's doing."

"She wants to see him herself. Bet you five bucks."

Marisa wasn't about to bet on it. The

old lover, father of her child — who could tell what Ruth might want?

Nick said, "You just think the guy's called Hartman. She knows his name — and where he lives. She'll go straight to him, zing! All we have to do is follow."

Marisa was silent.

"If you can think of a better way let's have it."

She couldn't, and although the idea of waiting bored her, and its practical application had also been a bore, she had to admit, right now, sitting in the station wagon at the intersection of Pine Grove and EastWest Drive, that the waiting game had paid dividends. All the same she said, wisely, "He wasn't there, she came out too quickly."

"OK. Then he lives some place else. All we have to do is find out where."

"Oh sure. Easy."

"Easier than walking into an office building and making up crazy stories."

"Did you see that gate, Nick? It's not the kind of gate where you go and say,

'We understand Mr Hartman doesn't live here, could you please give us his address?'"

He had to agree. She added, "Maybe I try the walking-in act again — see what happens."

"Oh God, Batwoman! No." (My reaction would have been apoplectic. She was considering the one move which could have proved disastrous, and which I'd dismissed as being out of the question.)

Marisa said, "Why not?"

His negative had been a gut reaction but he soon thought of reasons for it. "Julie Wrenn said he's rich as hell — he must be to own a place like that . . . "

She nodded.

"He'll have a wife and kids, and maybe they don't know about you being his little bastard."

That was also possible.

"You go storming in there right after your ma . . . For God's sake, Marisa, you're not the only one who can add two and two, you'd be asking for trouble. And like you say, he can't be there or she'd have stayed longer."

Marisa considered the facts; they made sense. Her mother had gone directly to this house, obviously to see him or find out where he was; she hadn't stayed more than twenty-five minutes, not long enough for that kind of reunion after so many years, therefore he hadn't been there. But the house was the connection, the vital link. Nick was right, as he often was; but not invariably, as time was about to demonstrate. She said, "We should've followed them when they left. She's probably talking to him right now."

"And we'd be fouled up in some traffic jam, you can't follow in a city."

"We made it here."

"Sure. Freeway, and then this one turn-off. No problem."

"So . . . what do we do?"

What they did was go to a Taco Bell for something to eat ("Not," Marisa said, "quite up to Uncle

Will's standard") and while they ate they considered. Eventually Nick said, "OK, how does this grab you? I turn up at the gate with a package addressed to Mr Scott Hartman — special delivery. Pity I don't have my Honda. You keep out of the way, back around that corner with the car. The guys on duty will say he doesn't live there. I'll tell 'em somebody goofed — so where *does* he live? And they redirect me."

"You think?"

"Sure. And if they don't, I can kind of lead around to it, can't I?" He wasn't as confident as he made himself sound, but he couldn't think of anything better. So they bought an envelope and created the 'package', and returned to EastWest Drive.

Just as he was about to set out, Marisa suddenly produced Cross-eye from her pocket and told him he must touch the smooth stone for luck. Nervous, he said, "Come on, don't let's screw around, let's do it." Perhaps things would have turned out differently if he'd done as she asked, but he wanted to move while he still had a few shreds of confidence.

Even so, there were butterflies in his stomach as he approached the guardhouse ('Like some goddam frontier out of a movie'), and he realized, too late, that the guys manning the frontier post weren't dummies; he could see two of them watching his approach, and had a feeling they could sense his lack of confidence at forty feet.

He said, "Package for Mr Scott Hartman."

"Who from?"

"Don't know, sir, they don't tell us."

The interviewing guard was tall and young, the near-uniform which had admitted us, I imagine. He took the package and looked at it thoughtfully, at the same time feeling its thickness: possibly to see if it might contain explosive. Somehow Nick had not expected them to be this professional, like cops. Perhaps the guard felt some sympathy for the nervous youngster, perhaps he had a kid brother, because he gave him an out: "No Mr Hartman here. Somebody got the wrong address, or maybe the wrong name."

Nick should have taken his package and gone while the going was temporarily good; but the thought of Marisa's ironical blue eye made him stick to his guns. "It's kind of urgent — where do I find him?"

"Well now," said the young guard, "I'd say that was none of your business. What outfit you with?"

Neither Nick nor Marisa had foreseen this one. He grabbed out of thin air the name of the only delivery firm he knew in Los Angeles — one of his high-school buddies worked for it part time: "Ace."

To his horror, the guard opened a reference directory, flipping to the As. "No Ace." His eyes were not at all friendly now — Nick felt his knees trembling. "So what's your game?"

"No game, sir, just delivering."

"Where's your bike, car?"

"Left it down the hill aways. Didn't look like there was parking up here."

The guard slipped a finger under the flap of the envelope and ripped it open. Nick's stomach dropped into his Nikes. Out of the envelope fell a Mobil street plan of Los Angeles, the only sufficiently weighty document they'd been able to find in the glove compartment.

The guard, stern-faced now, picked up a phone, pressed a number, and said, "Mr Lindsey. Sorry to disturb you, sir. Got a suspicious young guy down here — you said you wanted us to report."

There was then a sticky pause. A second guard appeared, stared at Nick and went out again. Presently the Maserati arrived and pulled to a halt, throbbing. The engine cut, and Mark Lindsey came into the room looking irritated. Like me, Nick had no doubt, from Marisa's description of him, that this was her 'Mr Greedy-lips'. The next few minutes were the most embarrassing of his young life; he and Marisa had never evolved a cover story so, to use his own words, "I had to play dumb, and every damn question I couldn't answer just dug me deeper in the shit." Lindsey and the guard grew increasingly exasperated. He didn't suppose the guard would resort to pulling off his fingernails one by one, but he wouldn't have put it past the boss. Neither would I. In the end, in a doom-ridden silence, he examined Nick's usually seraphic face intently; then held up the street plan. "You from LA?"

"Er . . . just happened to have it around, sir."

"Don't fuck with me. Know a lady called Adams? Mrs Ruth Adams?"

Nick had half expected this. "No, sir."

Lindsey nodded. Nick was surprised to notice, out of the depths of his own nervousness, that the man was oddly nervous too. He wondered why, but (like the rest of us) was as yet too ignorant of the whole complex situation to even guess at an answer.

After staring for a moment longer, Lindsey said to the guard, "Oh for Christ's sake! I don't have time to waste on this punk, neither do you. Hand him over to the police."

Nick says he stood paralyzed and open-mouthed.

"What charge, sir?"

"We'll talk about that." He jerked his head towards the door, and the two of them left the room.

Marisa, out of the station wagon by now and peering through a copse of dwarf pines, heard the approaching police car and thought, "Oh my God, it can't be!" But it was.

3

Something about our conversation *chez* Hartman had changed my attitude towards the whole situation: or, more subtly, I was now becoming more and more deeply involved in it, the usual result of trying one's hand at any kind of puzzle. I had been researching a complex novel in and around this town for one whole year, so there was little I didn't know about collecting information in Portland. I had gone to see Christina Hartman because Ruth and my curiosity had willed me to it; and the more I thought about my sister-in-law's motives the more convinced I became that facing the wife had, for her, been some kind of test, even if it was only a test of preconceived ideas. I hoped she was now satisfied. My own preconceived ideas had been confirmed: the woman was a bitch and not a very clever one.

But as far as I was concerned the way to find Scott Hartman — obviously he wasn't in Europe; Christina couldn't have told a convincing lie to save her life — was to go straight to my old friends Kingley-Crossman; and that was what we now did.

The office occupies a small Victorian house on the other side of the

Willamette, the east side, the rougher side. On the door is inscribed 'Kingley-Crossman' and under it 'Inquiries'. A passer-by might think that this was the inquiry office for Kingley-Crossman Carpet Cleaners, like the business on their left, or for Kingley-Crossman Welding, like the one on their right. Actually it means exactly what it says: Kingley-Crossman Inquiries. The precise extent of their inquiries I have never asked, but they're quite evidently far-reaching. The staff all seem to be young and well educated, possibly possessors of degrees who have found a new and lucrative outlet for intelligence; the single exception is an elderly man with a broken nose who looks like an ex-cop and may be the brains behind the whole thing and/or somebody's father.

The desk is manned by a girl of about twenty with the prettiest face you could wish to see and the fattest body — nothing uncommon in Oregon which should have a fat lady as its state symbol. Always cheerful, she said, "Hartman. Ought to be easy." She told us to come back at two o'clock, and after a sandwich and a cup of coffee that's what we did. Mike, a smiling but deathly pale young man with a shock of black hair and large glasses, and Gina, equally pale with perfect Pre-Raphaelite features and a Pre-Raphaelite dress to go with them, had done a Nexis search on the computer but, they said, "with rich people it's usually bullshit". So they gave us what they called 'a few immediates'.

The first, from the gossip page of the *Oregonian*, dated October 1974, deplored the fact that Scott Hartman no longer decorated the social scene with his attractive presence and good humor. It clearly implied that Mrs Scott Hartman, who was seen everywhere, wasn't an adequate substitute — Christina must have enjoyed that! There were one or two other snippets in the same mode. Mr Hartman, or perhaps his money, seemed to have been greatly missed.

Then there was a paragraph from an unnamed paper, dated 1983, reporting that Scott Hartman had arrived back from Europe and had promptly disappeared into 'the hideaway we used to hear so much about'. No mention of where it was, but, 'let's hope he makes the occasional social sortie, we could do with his company'. A social sortie implied that the hideaway was local. Warmer.

There were several short pieces describing, without much detail and certainly without any mention of his having been drunk, the automobile accident in 1986. One, dated seven months later, said that he was still in hospital or back in hospital, it wasn't clear which, with further complications. Any day now he would probably be discharged and would no doubt disappear from sight yet again. In conclusion the writer lamented, "The old order changeth . . . " It certainly doth.

Mike and Gina had managed to

find an architectural description of the hideaway; they apologized for its great age, it had been printed in 1979, in one of those 'Design and Living' sections to which some people are obviously addicted, others using them almost immediately to light the fire. It described 'the superb example of the best in modern design which Franz Wilder is creating on a hilltop between Cannon Beach and Neahkahnie, the ocean-view property to end them all.' The word 'hideaway' implies something small, modest, but this hideaway was designed to hide big money, and it was huge. Judging from the photographs, a little too clever as usual, the house looked overblown if not demented: far too many cantilevers, and white beams supporting nothing, far too many walkways, some crisscrossing like a freeway intersection, leading where? It certainly wasn't the kind of place, stuck out in the wilds, that Christina Hartman would have considered as even a tiny spoke of her social wheel

(Gainsborough's smiling minx would have burst out laughing to find herself hung there), but of course that was why her husband *had* chosen it.

Mike said, "Doesn't seem to be too far from Astoria. I guess you know it."

"How can he know it?" demanded Gina. "You can't see it, and nobody knows it's there."

She had remembered one of her mother's friends mentioning the place, ages ago. Taking a chance, she'd called the friend, who lived on the coast near Manzanita, and had actually caught her at home for her lunch hour — I tell you, those kids at Kingley-Crossman are hundred per cent bloodhounds. It seemed you couldn't really see the house at all unless you were in a boat out on the ocean when it looked, according to Gina's mother's friend, like 'some kind of modern coast-guard installation'.

"But," added Gina, "if you look up to your left, just after that tunnel by Arch Cape, you catch a peep of something white — oh my God, real high up. That's it."

Ruth, who had by now assessed the bloodhounds pretty accurately, said, "Of course the phone number won't be listed. Pity."

"Phone numbers," replied Gina, "are Meredith's big thing, he's a whizz."

We never got to meet Meredith — was he perhaps the old ex-cop or Dad? He certainly had the right connections, because Gina came back in less than fifteen minutes with the number written on a piece of paper. In a schoolmistressy voice which suited her, she said, "Mr Adams, we don't do this kind of thing" — waving the slip — "for just anybody, but you being an old client . . ."

I assured her that I was the soul of discretion.

"If you'd like to call from here there's an empty office. We'll bill you of course."

Ruth stood at the window of the empty office, gazing out at a dying monkey puzzle tree. Almost all varieties of flora seem to enjoy the Oregon climate — you never saw such azaleas, such roses — but monkey puzzles, so much loved by the Victorians, must be an exception. Having made up her mind about whatever was perplexing it, she smiled at me, picked up the phone and tapped out the number; it really was a considerable move, this seventeen-year-long step into the past.

When a voice answered, she said, "I may have got the wrong address, I'm looking for Mr Scott Hartman. Is he there?" A pause. "To tell you the truth he hasn't heard from me in years; it may be a bit of a shock. Let me introduce myself, would you mind?"

I said, "Shall I disappear?"

"Heavens, no." And after a moment, "Scott? I hope you're sitting down, this may be rather a surprise." She listened, and then burst out laughing. "No, no, that's incredible, I *can't* sound the same. But you're dead right."

He spoke for a while. Then she said,

"How did I find you? Oh . . . via friends — Scott, I'd like to come and see you. I have something important to tell you." Again she listened, keeping her eyes on me. "OK," she said, "why not? Mind if I bring a friend — well, he's not a friend, he's my brother-in-law." And after further listening, "What does right away mean when I'm in Portland? An hour and a half, two hours. Great. We'll come and share your sunset."

Replacing the phone, she shook her head, bemused. "My God, he sounded . . . frail. He recognized my voice, but I would never have recognized his. I've a feeling nobody quite knows the truth about that accident."

"Except Christina."

"Sure, but Christina wasn't saying, was she?"

* * *

South of Cannon Beach as far as Nahalem the coast highway continually surprises you with a series of sea- and beach-scapes, each more breathtaking than the last. Then things become tamer and sometimes downright ugly until after Newport. Needless to say the Hartman 'ocean-view property to end them all' was sited at approximately the most beautiful point, in a southwest-facing fold of the Coast Range; it was called Hawk Rock after the large hill or little mountain which stood above it.

Hartman had told Ruth to stop at the post office on the highway by Arch Cape and to say we were going to visit Mr Scott for the first time; this semi-pseudonym must also have been a kind of password, because it produced a printed map without which we would never have found the entrance to the place: up what appeared to be a standard logging road. Only after a mile and a half did we come to the inevitable electronic gate, indicating that some form of habitation might lie ahead. The map told us how to deal with the gate, but even then we didn't reach Hawk Rock and the next gate for another two miles during which the road climbed through a logging scar and several magnificent stands of old pine and hemlock which had mercifully been spared.

No point in wondering how any 'private citizen' could acquire land like this — county — or state-owned land, I later discovered. I suppose the Dollar Fairy waved her wand, and lo and behold . . . The house, when we reached it, looked like a liner stranded on a hilltop — the 1970s were not famous for architectural taste. From the bridge of the liner, high above, a small face gazed down at us. Without its owner pressing a button there was strictly no admittance, short of leaving your car and climbing the cliff, man-made, I think, on top of which the house sat. This person turned out to be a Filipino manservant, ageless and impassive as they invariably are, but with bright discerning eyes; he immediately introduced himself as Clemente. A certain ceremonious excitement in his manner seemed to indicate that visitors at Hawk Rock were rare.

I can't say that even a writer's curiosity made me want to be present at this lovers' reunion, but equally I was determined at least to take a look at Scott Hartman. To me, who had never seen him before, he was a pitiable surprise; Ruth must have been truly shocked, but her face never revealed a flicker of it; perhaps his changed voice had prepared her for anything.

We were shown into a large room which I found blindingly, uncomfortably white, with shafts of late sunlight lying across it in almost solid slabs. Out of this glare arose a long pale figure, at one with the whiteness and the light. He seemed to waver towards us, ghostlike, and in some senses a ghost he was. Scarecrow-thin under loose, pale clothes, specially designed to make him comfortable, I'm sure, he held out his arms to Ruth, and they hugged one another. She seemed to give herself entirely to this greeting but her face, as she turned from him, revealed for an instant how difficult she had found it.

Yet when one looked at him more closely he wasn't the skeleton wraith he had first appeared to be. Too thin, yes, but in some ways quite healthy, palely tanned, a little color on his cheeks where surgery had not left too many white scars. Hands usually reveal a person's true build, and his were big: 'sensitive' hands as they say, and in that context his face was sensitive too. In spite of suffering, his brown eyes had not lost the vital spark; his hair was pale, fairly long, mostly white but with shadows of what had once been brown. If he was the ghost of a man, the man in question had been good-looking, humorous, intelligent — I found myself quickly revising some of my misconceptions. His right arm was permanently bent, and his right leg was in some esoteric way artificial; the whole body was twisted and, I think, gave him occasional, perhaps continual, pain. Ruth had told me he was now sixty-one years old, he could have been ten, twenty years older.

After being introduced I excused myself, saying how eager I was to look at the house and its rocky but evidently designed surroundings. Ruth later recounted their conversation, quietly, without emphasis; I think she needed to recount it as an act of exorcism.

He said, "OK, I'm a wreck. You know what happened."

"Automobile crash."

"Putting it mildly. I was coming down here. I'd had a few drinks, more than a few. Lost control, hit the parapet of one of those bridges on Sunset Highway — you must have passed it on your way down, Burnt Creek. Thank God no one else was involved."

"Did you . . . ? I didn't notice Burnt Creek — did you go through?"

"A hundred and seventy-four feet."
And, wryly, "They always measure.
Somehow I fell out before the tank
went up, full tank. No, no . . . " He
waved attenuated hands. "You don't
have to react, I'm just telling you
— I'm long past sympathy, all that."

"And you were in hospital a long
time. I know, a friend wrote me."

"In and out for nearly three years."

He had drawn her to the group
of chairs where he'd been sitting;
they came with the house, looked
like giant cats' cradles but were
surprisingly comfortable. He gazed at
her as they sat down, and said, "Oh
Ruth, Ruth!" She felt an awkwardness
between them, unimaginable at one
time, long ago. It distressed her, and
in her distress she began to talk, trying
to keep awkwardness at bay. She told
him about her marriage, Jack's work.
He said, "Sounds like a nice guy, I'm
glad."

"The nicest."

"Rare in that business." He spread

both bony hands. "In any business, I guess."

Embarrassing silence came stalking them again. She asked, "Do you live here alone?"

"I'm looked after by wonderful people."

"Like your Filipino."

"Clemente's the best of them." He made a face. "If you mean alone alone . . . The accident put paid to women — not that I cared, after . . . Not that I care."

Grasping at straws, Ruth told him how her acting career had been unable to compete with marriage, and how easily she had been able to give it up. It was a few minutes before she realized that he, sitting against that blaze of light, was silently weeping. For a moment panic seized her, the effect naked emotion has on many of us; but this is an experienced and intelligent woman, as well as a compassionate one, and she suddenly understood that they would never be able to carry on an ordinary conversation; this was the meaning of the impending, threatening silence. What had once been between them, and what had subsequently happened to him, made ordinary conversation impossible.

She told me that only then did she remember my remark over dinner the night before, about their relationship having been 'gorgeous old sex', and she realized with a sense of loss that this was *all* it had been; they'd had little enough in common seventeen years ago, and now they had virtually nothing. The thought seemed to her so sad, 'brutally sad' was her phrase, that she was speechless; but then, sensible woman, she came straight to the point of her visit; that, at least, was something they shared. She said, "Scott, my dear, I hope you aren't going to be mad at me."

"Ruth, was I ever?"

"Yes, frequently, towards the end. Christina made sure of that."

As if even the name disgusted him,

he turned his head abruptly aside.

"You see . . . I held out on you."

"Is this what you meant on the phone, you had something important to tell me?"

"Yes. Right at the end, when I went to LA, I was pregnant."

He leaned forward and put his head in his hands; she hoped he wasn't again in tears. Like most of us she found them impossible to cope with; all you can do is go to the person and hold them, and somehow she didn't want to, wouldn't have known how to, hold that twisted, perhaps pain-racked, body. But he wasn't in tears; he said, "One thing I've learned in the past nine years is never to use the word 'if'."

"Even 'if' would have made no difference, I'd have gone anyway. I had to go, she'd made anything else impossible."

"I could . . . should have gone with you."

"Should you, Scott? I don't think so. We . . . We'd had our time and it was wonderful. Until the end."

"Bitch! They should have certified me before they let me marry her."

"So," said Ruth, "we have a daughter."

"Beautiful?"

"She will be — very."

"What's her name?"

"Marisa."

"Pretty name." And after a moment, "Does she know?"

"We had to tell her Jack wasn't her father, we always meant to. And of course she wanted to meet her real father right away."

"You didn't tell her who I was?"

"No."

He frowned as if puzzled. "And she wants to meet me?" "Wouldn't you, at seventeen?"

"I don't know. Men are different."

"She . . . did a little detective work, and came up here to find you. I followed — I couldn't bear the idea of her bursting in on you when . . . when you didn't even know she'd happened."

184

"Yes, that would have been a shock."

Ruth recalled that she had wanted to prevent Marisa meeting this man. Why? Not only because he'd have been shocked by the fact of her existence; there seemed to have been more than that, but the reason now evaded her. She said, "You'll see her, won't you?"

"Heavens, yes — nothing would stop me. I never get to see any pretty girls these days." He smiled, making a rueful face which brought back intimate, sunlit memories. "As a matter of fact, one came here a couple of weeks ago. Beautiful creature. Tried to interview me for some scandal sheet. Staff had to throw her out." At once, Ruth thought of her daughter's reception when she had walked into the Hartman offices with her 'school project'. She investigated with care: "Don't you give interviews?"

"Hell, no! So off she went, this gorgeous gal, and talked to all the old women of both sexes — and came up with a piece about how much I disliked

185

my family and how scared they all were about not getting the money. Oh my God, a real load of dirt." He chuckled. "The family weren't amused."

Least of all, thought Ruth, Mr Mark Lindsey. Yes, that would have been enough to make him see the media hiding under every table. He confirmed her thought by adding, "I never go near Hartman any more. It's run by the appalling guy Susan decided to marry."

Her own memory of Lindsey prompted her to ask, "Why appalling?"

"Operator. Came from Phoenix. After her money of course. But she's as bloody-minded as her mother; she was determined to have him. Now . . . She's not so crazy about him now."

Ruth hadn't mentioned the visit to his wife, to his old home, because she knew that any account of Christina's words and behavior would upset him. His brief moment of humor had now faded; he was lying back in his cat's cradle as if exhausted. After a moment, in a drained voice, he said, "Oh God, Ruth, if only my boy had lived, my Tom."

They were both silent, thinking of the drowned son: one of the few people who had ever made his life worth living. Ruth knew that she herself was another, maybe the only other, but she could never have stayed with him; it would never have worked out. He said, "When will you bring her here, tomorrow?"

"I hope so. She's avoiding me."

"Why?"

"She thinks I want to stop her meeting you. I did — as I explained. But it'll be OK now." Again that evasive doubt taunted her; she dismissed it impatiently. They had fallen into another long silence. She says she could almost feel the last drops of what had once united them, so violently and exclusively, trickling away like the last of the water in a desert; the thirsty ground absorbed it, and the sun scorched out every last trace. Eventually, resorting to present reality and mere social convention, all that appeared to be left to them, he said, "We ought to call your tactful brother-in-law. Time for a drink."

He rang a bell and asked Clemente to find me. I came in, dazed by sun and sky and the vast distances which surrounded that rich man's retreat, dazed also by the numbing banality of the sprawling house. I was surprised to recognize intense relief in Ruth's welcome: no, not perhaps surprised, but once again saddened. We had drinks, beautifully prepared by Clemente, accompanied by his wife's canapés — she was obviously a remarkable cook. Then, I'm sorry to say, we made our escape as soon as was decently possible: conversation had tended to flag, even with me around, an unusual circumstance. His acceptance of our wish to escape was in itself heart-rending. Remembering my sardonic remarks at his expense, with regard to inherited wealth and its effect on the recipients, I was ashamed of myself; and yet I couldn't help feeling that another kind of man, his own thrusting great-grandfather for instance, in whom the juices of life had run rich and strong, would have found a different, more useful, and far from reclusive, way to spend the rest of his days.

He came out onto the main deck of the stranded liner and watched as we descended flights of white wooden stairs towards my car. He said, "You've got the number. Let me know when you're bringing the girl — well in advance."

Ruth looked back and up at him, shading her eyes against the glare. "Of course. Tomorrow with any luck."

"I'm looking forward to it."

We had reached the car and were both just about to get into it when he added, almost as a throwaway line, "Who knows, maybe I'll make her my heir."

★ ★ ★

We didn't speak of this, we didn't speak of anything, until long after we'd been let out of the top gate and were making our way down the winding road towards the second one. The sun was descending between lowering bastions of gray-purple cloud to its nightly drowning in the Pacific: a harsh, melodramatic sunset. Ruth glanced at me. "You heard of course."

"Yes, I heard."

"Will, he *couldn't*."

"He could. Whether or not he would . . . "

She pressed both hands to her face; she was wondering if it was this, some strange premonition of this, which had from the beginning made her want to keep them apart. But as we drove down the hillside, passing through deep groves of conifer which even the setting sun couldn't pierce, she only said, "No. It's impossible."

I didn't answer; whatever else it

might be it was not impossible. I said, "If he really hates his wife that much . . . But maybe he doesn't, not any more."

"He couldn't even bear it when I mentioned her name."

"But," I said, beginning to recognize the depth of her distress, "his wife isn't next of kin, that would be the silly daughter."

"He doesn't think much of her either. And he can't stand his son-in-law."

"Good taste." In the end I'd probably find myself liking Scott Hartman.

She said, "Will, if I thought he was serious, if I thought he'd really do anything so . . . monstrous, I'd take Marisa home. Right now."

"She wouldn't go, she'd disappear again. And even if you did, back she'd come like a boomerang — she wants to see him more than anything in the world."

She was silent.

"Don't you remember the passionate wants of seventeen?"

"Oh God! Too well."

"You can't stop her meeting him, Ruth; it would be counter productive."

She turned her head away and looked out of the window, not seeing anything, I'm sure. I was wondering to what extent that meeting, particularly in view of Hartman's last equivocal remark, constituted the moment I'd been waiting for, the moment when danger made its presence known. It didn't take a genius to visualize the effect of Hartman's words if they could have been heard at Number Seven, EastWest Drive. I said, "After she's seen him, got it out of her system, maybe that *would* be the time to take her home."

"I'm beginning to wish we'd never told her. Then none of this could have happened." An honest person facing the results of her own honesty, my heart went out to her. But I also thought that perhaps we were making the worst of things, looking on the blackest side. I tried, "To tell you the truth, it didn't sound to me as if he really meant it — more of an ironical joke."

She shook her head. "I know the accident's changed him utterly, but . . . I can't quite see Scott making that kind of joke. I wish I could."

4

When Marisa saw Nick being led out of the Hartman blockhouse, saw him being introduced to the police, she was at first so stunned that her brain seized up — but only for a few seconds, because she turned, ran back to her station wagon and was sitting at the wheel, engine running, by the time the police car began its return journey. As it passed the end of Pine Grove she pulled out and followed. It seemed to her essential to discover, at the very least, which precinct her best friend was being taken to.

As anybody who has ever tried following another car in city traffic will know, every intersection is a death-defying challenge, every light an enemy. She realized that Nick had been right: only the fact that we'd stayed on the freeway until the required exit had made it possible for them to follow my Taurus all the way from Astoria to the mansion on the hill. Within a few minutes she had not only lost the police car, she was hopelessly lost herself. Portland is only a small city, but it has a system of one-way streets which can catch a stranger unawares and hold him like a fly in honey. When she finally found a place to park, and when she finally found a phone in good working order, she called my apartment for the first time. Two hours had passed since I'd driven away with her mother; if we'd gone back to Astoria we would by now have arrived there. No answer.

It seemed to her that EastWest Drive must be part of a specific police district, but she was by then a long way from it, with no idea of how to find it again — she wasn't very good when it came to direction, and left such things to Nick, if he was around. She tried asking at a gas station, but the only men she could find there didn't even know where EastWest Drive was located, and it was obviously their policy to keep as far away from the police as possible; her questions earned her some very funny looks.

Anxiety and her own determined character drove her to keep asking. The most sensible answer, given to her several times, was that the only people who could tell her what she wanted to know were the police themselves — look, wasn't that a police car parked over there in that mall? Her unwillingness to approach the guardians of the law directly earned her another round of funny looks. She reasoned that the last thing she could afford was to alert more policemen; she'd probably end up in the cooler herself, and not the same cooler as her best friend either.

Once she found time to consider the situation more closely, and she had plenty of time for that, further complications began to multiply in her mind. For instance, supposing she *did* discover where he was, what was she going to say, what was she expected to say, and what, of the many things she might say, would land her in trouble herself? And wasn't there something called bail? If they wanted her to bail him out she was sure she didn't have enough money.

Poor Marisa! It was the kind of predicament which would have confused a knowledgeable adult, and when it comes to police procedure most adults, as she was discovering the hard way, are far from knowledgeable. She found herself fighting tears of anger and frustration. She even got mad at her soapstone talisman which was proving worse than useless in this emergency. Clutching it, she called my number again — and again — and again. No answer of course; Ruth and I were up there in the forests of the Coast Range, or in that misfit house which looked like a liner stranded on top of a hill. When we finally got back to the apartment, still reeling from Scott Hartman's parting shot, Marisa was calling for the zillionth time.

I grabbed the phone. Ruth, after eavesdropping on the basic facts, stood lost in thought while I tried to talk her daughter down. Rain was billowing across the Columbia, lashing the surface to a dull steely gray. Seals were honking near, or under, one of the remaining fish canneries, waiting for leftovers. When she'd finished thinking she relieved me of the phone and said, "Listen, darling. Why did the police take him?" She shook her head in disbelief. "Yes, I see. And where is this café you're in? Corner of . . . Gleason." She wrote it down, looking at me. I nodded, I knew it. "Of course we'll come up, just sit tight. And Marisa, get off the line now, I have to make a couple of calls."

The incisive manner was not natural to her, she'd had to learn it from experience as Jack had climbed the ladder of success: irritated producers who were afraid he was going over budget, wheedling actresses who wanted lines changed, apologetic editors who seemed to have mislaid Scene 99, Take 9. I watched her open her purse and find Scott Hartman's phone number, neatly written on the slip of paper given to us by Pre-Raphaelite Gina. Our eyes met. She said, "I guess this is where we use our influential friends. You'd better tune in."

I went to the extension in my bedroom, remembering that before the visit to Hawk Rock we'd decided not to mention our morning's activities in Portland — which meant that she now had some awkward explaining to do.

"Scott, it's Ruth."

"You can't find her. Tomorrow's off."

"No, not at all. I've spoken to her; I know where she is. When we met I didn't tell you I'd been to Number Seven this morning."

"For God's sake! What for?"

"I thought you might be there. And if you weren't, I thought . . . hoped she'd tell me where you were."

"Ingenuous of you. All you got was some prime bitching, right?"

"A little, but I expected it. The point is, our daughter followed me; I said she was trying to find you."

"Seems I'm a popular guy."

"And, Scott, the boy who was with her got arrested by the men at the gate."

"Arrested! What the hell for?"

"Asking questions. And they . . . well, I gather it was Mark Lindsey, handed him over to the police."

Anything his family did would probably anger him. I'd expected him to be angry, but not to the extent he now was. Deafened by his rage, I didn't find it too easy to think clearly myself, but I suddenly had a nasty feeling that Nick's fortuitous, somewhat absurd, adventure was having an effect out of all proportion to its real significance.

Ruth may have been feeling the same because she said, "Please, Scott, it isn't really very important."

"Let me be the judge of that."

"I'm calling you because we don't know where the police took this boy — he's practically a young man. If you could possibly locate him . . . "

"Of course I can. That's my home, for God's sake — I spent forty years of my life there. As for Lindsey . . . "

"I expect he was only doing what he thought was his duty."

"He wouldn't know his duty from his ass."

"And please . . . Listen to me, Scott. Don't mention Marisa being . . . our child."

"Why not? Do you think I'm ashamed of it?"

"You'll only upset them."

"Hell to them, let them be upset."

"But there's no need . . . "

"Ruth, you've asked me to help and I will. Don't tell me what I need or needn't do with my own damn family.

I'll call you back. About a half-hour."

I replaced the extension thoughtfully and went into the living room. Ruth was staring down at the phone. I said, "Looks like you started something."

"What else could we do, Will?"

"Nothing. We seem to have a foot caught in it, don't we?"

There was no way of knowing whether loss of temper had done him any physical harm — in his pitiable condition it was hard to say what might or might not harm him — but it was Clemente who called back three-quarters of an hour later. He was sorry, Mr Hartman couldn't come to the phone right now, but he had taken care of everything; he gave us the address of the police precinct in question and the name of the officer we should ask for when we got there.

Ruth said, "Clemente, is he all right?"

"Mr Scott tired. Easy tired. Rests now. He says you want anything more you call us right away."

So, once more, we began the ninety-mile journey back to Portland. For a long time we were both silent, occupied with our own thoughts. Eventually Ruth said, "You were right. We seem to have got a foot caught in it."

"Creatures of circumstance. Can't be helped — all we can do is accept our fate and see it through."

She laid a hand on my arm. "Dear Will. You'll be glad to see the back of us."

"Not at all. Haven't had so much action in years."

"I know you too well to buy that. You're like me — anything for a quiet life."

It sounded boring, but she was right. Marisa's arrival — was it really only forty-eight hours ago? It seemed like a week! — had been a rock hurled into the calm pool where writers like to sit; the ordinary business of living had been swamped by troubled waves, not lessened by Nick's recent endeavors. I'd given up hankering after chapter nine — it was going to be a long time before I finished that truncated sentence — but what about more practical matters? The refrigerator was almost empty — I doubted if there was anything for tomorrow's breakfast — and hadn't I arranged for my car, still under guarantee, to be serviced? I hoped I'd written it down in the diary. And, my God, where were we all going to sleep tonight? The apartment would burst at the seams.

The rush hour was over by the time we reached Portland; downtown had settled into its evening inertia. In common with many other big cities, it was abandoned at the end of the working day, everyone retiring to the dormitory satellites where they could find all they needed in the way of food and drink and entertainment.

We liberated Marisa from solitary confinement in the café; earlier she'd grown weary of discouraging male attention, the place was much used by young executives, but that had been a lot more entertaining than sitting there on her own. She was very relieved to see us. Once again the pendulum had swung, and she seemed younger than her years, and not, I thought, quite so sure of herself. Every encounter with the sandpaper of life rubs off a little self-assurance — one of the prices we all pay for growing up.

She immediately asked, "Did you find him? I knew he wasn't at that huge house, you weren't in there long enough."

"Yes, we found him." I could see Ruth coming to terms with the fact that the rest had to be said, whatever her doubts: those doubts which she couldn't quite understand herself. "He wants to see you."

Marisa was delighted, but a shadow lay behind the delight. "When?"

"Tomorrow."

I knew what the girl was feeling. We've all experienced that eager, blinkered looking forward to a thing, and then the sudden drop of the stomach when there's nothing between you and what you've so passionately wanted. She echoed it almost unbelievingly: "Tomorrow."

When we left the café, which was on the point of closing, she drove with her mother in the station wagon and I led them to the police precinct. Hartman's designated officer, a sergeant, was middle-aged and overweight, with one of those pasty police faces and hooded eyes which held mine a shade too directly: odd how this is either a sign of genuine candor or genuine dishonesty, seldom anything between. He said, "We're not too happy about this, I'm here to tell you."

I was slightly taken aback. "I thought Mr Hartman — "

"Mr Hartman's an old friend; we always try to oblige him. But an ounce of crack ain't too easy to overlook."

I'm afraid I gaped. While I was doing so Nick was escorted into the office, which smelled of stale sweat and disinfectant as they invariably do. He looked surly, scared.

I pulled myself together and lied. "Officer, I've known this young man for years; he never touches drugs."

Nick erupted. "I told 'em, I told 'em a hundred times, it's strictly for goofs."

"So what were you aiming to do with it?" snapped the sergeant. "Sell?"

"Somebody planted it." He turned to me. "Must have been the guy on the gate, Will — he frisked me."

The sergeant groaned. "If I had a buck for every young jerk I've heard say that."

Nick ignored him and continued: "He said to Lindsey, 'What charge?' and Lindsey said they'd talk about that outside . . . "

"You'd better watch what you say about Mr Lindsey too."

This was obviously a situation which had to be met head-on. I said, "OK, let's stop messing around. Mr Hartman told me personally he'd arranged for this release."

Bottom line — ambivalent police authority wavering. "All I can say, the kid's darn lucky to have important friends."

"Nobody's arguing with that. Can we go?"

"Guess so."

Nick erupted again: "Will, I swear — " I grabbed his arm and held it so tightly he winced. Then I looked directly into the dishonest eyes. "Thank you, officer. I'm sure Mr Hartman will be giving you proof of his gratitude." And I lugged my charge out of the building.

Later, in Thank God It's Friday, which seemed to be the right place to eat after that incoherent day, he said, "Land of the free, my foot; it's a police state. And Lindsey's a dip-shit!" A glance at Ruth: "Sorry."

"Don't apologize, he is."

Marisa looked at me, frowning. "I don't get it. Nick doesn't mean a thing to them."

"It was a warning, and a heavy

warning too. Your mother can tell you why."

"Some journalist-woman tried to interview Scott. She was thrown out, and wrote a load of spiteful garbage. So when you walked into that office Lindsey thought you were another one." She shook her head. "It's a good thing he didn't know who you really were."

"Then," I continued, "along comes Mrs Ruth Adams, trying to find Scott Hartman. And on top of that they get Nick, also trying to find Scott Hartman."

Marisa spread both hands. "So what's wrong with people wanting to see him?"

I caught Ruth's eye; we were both thinking of that quiet, hoarse voice: "Who knows, maybe I'll make her my heir."

"It's all to do with the money, Marisa. He *is* the money, he's the power. He cracks the whip and they dance."

She said, "I hate that kind of money, it's ugly."

"OK, it's ugly, but it's their god. Now something they don't understand seems to be threatening it — and them."

"Nobody's threatening them."

Only you, I thought, and you don't even know it. But I said, "They think they're being threatened, and they're scared. And when rich people run scared they throw their weight around."

"Proving what?"

"Proving they have the power to do what they like — and the law isn't about to stop them."

This made Ruth glance away, biting her lip. She was thinking that if the Hartmans had been scared before, they'd be even more scared now, following Scott's intervention on Nick's behalf. In his rage he would certainly have ignored her asking him not to mention Marisa; in fact I was sure it would give him savage satisfaction to let them know he had an illegitimate daughter. I'd wondered if the level of radiation might become critical while our attention was elsewhere, and by God it had. Worse still, we seemed to be stuck with it behind locked doors — no escape.

★ ★ ★

By the time we got back to Astoria, yet again, we were almost too weary to tackle the reorganization of our sleeping arrangements: Nick into the junk room where he fell asleep instantly amid the rubbish I couldn't bear to throw away; Ruth retaining the guest room; Marisa appropriating my bed and pushing me onto the sofa which, thank heaven, is long and comfortable.

She and her mother had been calling Jack, using the only extension beside my vacated bed. When they had finished Ruth came to me and said, "Will, I'm not going with you when you take Marisa to see Scott tomorrow."

I wasn't surprised, and I thought I

knew her reasons, but all the same I asked, "Why not?"

"I think the sight of me . . . pressures him. He starts remembering, and that makes him angry. I figure it'll be easier if I'm not around." No doubt she was also thinking of his last unsettling words, and wanted at all costs to cool the whole overheated situation. She said, "That was pretty ugly, what they did to Nick."

"I've a feeling they can get a lot uglier if they choose. I wish to hell you could take Marisa home right away."

"Not a hope. Seeing him is the most important thing in her life, the ruling passion."

And if the ruling passion wasn't satisfied she'd continue her quest until it was — possibly alone, and that was something which mustn't be allowed to happen. In my simplicity I'd imagined that Connie's precipice was situated at Number Seven, EastWest Drive; maybe it once was but now it had moved, and Marisa was still on the edge of it; moreover the motives for somebody giving her that fatal push were getting stronger.

Ruth said, "We can't do a thing, not until they've met."

"And then?"

Her face fell into lines of sadness. "I think it's going to be a disaster, Will. I think she's heading for a really shattering disappointment."

Sad, yes, and harsh; but it was our best, perhaps our only, hope of escape.

★ ★ ★

Before going to bed I have a habit of checking the window in the hall outside my apartment. One rainy night it was left open, and I had to pay for the ensuing damage. Just as I was turning away from it something in the street below caught my eye: a black Dodge pick-up parked at the opposite curb. When you've lived in a town for a while you get used to the same vehicles parked in the same place night after night, but this wasn't one I'd seen before. I might not have noticed it at all if it hadn't been for Marisa and Nick's alarming experience on the freeway. I didn't of course think that this was the same pick-up, it didn't have mountain wheels for a start, but the association of ideas was what made me look at it more closely.

I was just dismissing it as belonging to a neighbor's guest when there was a tiny flare of light from the cab: tiny, but enough to reveal the bearded man who had just lit a cigarette, taking care to shield the flame. Was he merely waiting for somebody (a bit late for that, Astoria goes to bed early)? In which case why take precautions with his lighter? Or was he watching the house?

It had been a crowded and exhausting day; so much unfamiliar action, so many odd experiences, had perhaps acclimatized me to the unexpected, and by God I was tired. So there might or might not be a man watching the house — so good luck to him and to hell with him — he could even get to see a cat if he was lucky.

I double-locked the front door and staggered to my makeshift bed. I may have wondered if there was anything intelligent I ought to have done about the man outside, but I can't have come to any conclusion — I was asleep within five minutes.

4

Hawk Rock

1

RUTH and Marisa talked for a long time next morning, starting in the guest room and continuing over breakfast at the table in the bay window. Beyond them the Columbia was misty gray, the Washington hills were striated with layers and veils of low cloud, and the bridge faded away as if terminating itself in mid-stream. Downriver where visibility must have been worse a big ship was bellowing at regular intervals, impressing her presence on any other craft in the vicinity. The sound added to the tension which was coiled around the apartment, like a boa constrictor trying to crush it to death.

I steered Nick into the kitchen where we ate our own breakfast and read newspapers in companionable masculine silence; though at one point he did look up, frowning, and say, "Is this going to be OK, Will, this meeting with Bio-Dad?"

Neither he nor Marisa had any idea that there could be massive complications. I was sure Ruth wasn't enlightening her daughter, and I wasn't about to enlighten Nick. I said, "Let's hope so. There's sure as hell no way of stopping it." Something in my tone made him examine me more sharply — he doesn't miss much.

He hadn't missed the fact that my paper headlined yet another shock-horror story about AIDS: another miracle cure had failed. Feeling his eyes on me, I looked up from it; he grimaced.

"Can't be much fun," I said.

"Sure isn't."

"How do you get by?"

"You don't — 'less you're crazy. I

216

don't anyway. I guess I'm, you know, kind of celibate."

"There's some idea it's educated into you and can be educated out."

"Hogwash. I fell in love with the boy next door when I was eight, before they even dropped. You are or you're not — why don't they just leave it alone?"

I said, "Maybe they can't — Gay Rights and so on."

"Jeeze, they make me sick. So they're wannabe politicians, why don't they go for politics?" He drank some coffee and added, "Can get kind of lonely though. If I didn't have Marisa I guess I'd flip."

"In the end she'll probably meet Mr Right — one way or another."

"Don't tell me. Maybe I'll meet Mr Right too, and join the rat race."

"Those things can last."

"Never seen it myself, but then I live in LA where nothing lasts."

"At least you're honest with yourself — that's half the battle."

"Half? You think?"

I shrugged. He grinned.

Ruth had already called Hawk Rock and arranged a time with Clemente, ten o'clock, but Marisa and I left early, giving ourselves room for error; you never know with fog on that coast, from Alaska to Southern California it can play all kinds of tricks.

Seeing us off, Ruth said, "I'll call again in a few minutes and say I'm not coming."

"He'll want to know the reason."

"How about a virus? Nobody needs a virus in that house."

If useless Andy Swensen had waylaid us on our way out with any of his imbecile chatter I think, on that particular morning, I'd have strangled him; but he doesn't like damp weather, says it gets him in the chest. If that's the case he's living in the wrong state and had better move quickly; none of the tenants would stop him.

When we were crossing Young's Bay Bridge I said, "Your mother briefed you pretty thoroughly by the look of it."

Marisa nodded. "Is he . . . ? Was he badly hurt in that accident?"

"Yes. He's a wreck — looks at least fifteen years older than he is."

"He's much older than her anyway."

"Not unusual."

"I know. Some of the girls at school . . . Older men don't do a thing for me."

"Long may it last; they're usually trouble."

After a long pause, a mile-and-a-half pause, she asked, "Why did seeing him again make her so unhappy?"

"Partly the accident, I think. And going back is usually a big mistake. The house you thought was a mansion when you were a kid turns out to be a shack."

"Same with people, huh?"

"As far as I'm concerned. Nostalgia's a disease; I stay away from it."

There was another long silence, only a mile this time. Then: "I *have* to see him, Will. You understand, don't you?"

"I told you I did. I still do."

"Just once, that's all."

I hoped it would be all. She added, "I wish Mom had come with us."

"Quite a switch! You rushed up here without even telling her where you were going."

"You'll help me out, won't you?"

"I'll come in for a minute or two. He won't want me there and neither will you."

She grimaced. "I'm scared, and that's crazy."

"The whole thing's a bit crazy, Marisa, but we're stuck with it, aren't we?"

She glanced out of the window, suddenly angry. "Oh God, *why* did they have to tell me?" She had said it before, but this time, when she was on the verge of meeting him, it sounded like actual regret. Evenly and quietly I also repeated myself: "They're honest, and they love you, Marisa.

Some people might have kept quiet. I don't know, it's a tricky one."

We had passed Seaside and were approaching the Portland turn-off where Highway 26 leaves the coast road. The two vehicles behind us both headed for Portland, which is why I noticed for the first time the vehicle which had previously been behind them. It was a black pick-up. The one I'd seen parked outside my apartment? There are a thousand black pick-ups around. Following us? Or just using the coast road as we were? How could I tell? I couldn't even see if the driver had a beard.

The weather had been clearing as we went south, but once we were over the hump of Tillamook Head we were back in heavy sea mist. Occasional sunlight flashed through, with strange secretive glimpses of the Pacific looking innocently blue, the mood in which it drowns people. By the time we left the highway and began twisting and turning up into the forested hills, forested except for smears of logging vandalism, the black pick-up had disappeared. All around us the smaller deciduous bushes were putting on early fall coloring, patches of fire against dark dripping hemlocks. A deer bounded away from us into deep shadow. Marisa now sat very still, hardly seeming to breathe.

Glancing up, I was amazed to see the impossible house bathed in sunshine; presumably the very rich make their own arrangements with the Almighty regarding weather. Marisa leaned forward, staring. No comment. We topped the fat soft banks of fog, stretching as far as the eye could see to north and south, hugging the coastline; apart from them, the ocean was clear to the horizon. Above us Clemente raised a hand in greeting. The gate swung slowly open, and I drove in, parking under one of the cantilevers; here on Olympus, home of the gods, the sun was hot and would become hotter.

As we followed Clemente, climbing

wide steps to the liner's upper deck, I noticed that Cross-eye, the worry toad, had appeared in the girl's hand. We walked along a pointless corridor, all glass on the ocean side, the other hung with, to me, pointless paintings by people like Klee and Mondrian; I didn't suppose that Hartman liked them much either. They fitted their wall spaces too neatly, as if some once-fashionable decorator of the seventies had ordered them by the yard. Clemente tapped on a door, then admitted us to another vast room, one I hadn't previously seen. It was V-shaped, if you please — the apex of the stranded liner's superstructure.

Far away, Hartman was leaning at a window, staring out at the sparkling Pacific beyond the fog bank. Once again, emaciation and the fearful brightness of that over-windowed house made him look weirdly insubstantial. At that distance, pensively gazing, he seemed to be inhabiting some other world; gave a heart-catching impression of absolute, impenetrable aloneness;

but the charming smile transformed his face as he turned, and the eyes, which seemed to belong to another man trapped inside the smashed body, were warm and bright.

"Well," I said, "here we are. Mr Scott Hartman, Miss Marisa Adams. There's not much more I can add, is there?"

He said, "Why don't you stay and have a cup of coffee with us?" but he was only being polite.

"No thanks. I think I'll go to the upper deck and sit in the sun." The nautical reference made him smile; perhaps he didn't like his house any more than I did — only the isolation it afforded him. So I left them to their strange meeting.

I found some luxurious loungers encircling a kind of fountain on what would have been the roof, if any conventional word could have been applied to the place. A frog, or perhaps another toad, companion to Marisa's talisman, spewed water onto a large lily pad of green marble which in turn sent it splashing into a circular basin: the most civilized thing I'd yet seen at Hawk Rock. There was no point in worrying or wondering about what might transpire between father and daughter; we'd placed our bets and the great croupier in the sky had given the wheel a twist; in due time the little ball would rattle onto whatever number had been selected for it by fate. So I lay back and enjoyed the hilltop sunshine, high above the rest of the world's weather, listening to water and the wind in the pine trees. There should have been birdsong too, but I seldom hear any in Oregon, only a variety of chirps and the screaming of blue jays. Since they're surrounded by thousands of uninhabited acres they doubtless prefer to keep as far away as possible from *Homo*, sometimes called *sapiens*.

It wasn't much of a meeting when you considered the agonies and dissensions preceding it. A little more than forty minutes later, Clemente came to find me, expressing great disappointment that I hadn't asked for a drink; he said he mixed the best gin sling this side of Singapore, and I didn't doubt him.

If Ruth had seemed relieved to see me the day before, it was nothing to her daughter's reaction when I now reappeared. She even moved impulsively towards me, and then, well-raised girl that she is, decided that too great a show of relief would seem rude; but her expression said it all. What was it about the poor man which made people so eager to escape from his company? It was nothing to do with his appearance. Perhaps none of us properly understood how completely he had cut himself off from his fellow-human beings; like the proverbial castaway on a desert island he had lost the habit of easy speech, no longer knew how to accomplish it. Or was there some deeper reason? Did the raging dissatisfaction and anger he carried in his sick body reach out to some similar demon which lurks in all of us — dormant perhaps but still there? Were we in fact afraid of him as one is afraid of a leper, or his modern counterpart, HIV man?

He himself also seemed to have been strongly affected by this brief encounter, but in a negative, almost a defeated, way. He looked exhausted, shattered, and the warm brightness of his eyes, which had struck me as remarkable only a short time before, had become dulled as if by boredom. I saw Clemente give him a surreptitious, appraising look, the look a mother might bestow upon a delicate problem child.

He said, "Marisa's promised to come and see me again. This time she's going to bring her mother. I hope you'll come too." It was a mere pleasantry, a convention. He sounded as if our return was the last thing he wanted, and I suddenly wondered whether Ruth and I hadn't been constructing mountains out of molehills, seeing dragons where there were only little harmless lizards: in which case that throwaway remark about changing his will had been nothing but the wry joke I'd first considered it. Naturally he'd wanted to meet his illegitimate daughter, perhaps as eagerly as she had wanted to meet him. And that was all.

I could see Marisa wondering (a) whether she ought to kiss him goodbye and (b) if so, just how it might be achieved. Luckily he too had seen it coming and, after gripping a chairback for balance, leaned forward as much as he dared while she reached up and pecked his cheek.

When we were halfway down the hill her first words were, "His skin felt just like paper, Will. Thin, thin paper." And, after a moment's thought: "What does he do, all alone up there?"

"I think he sits and regrets his life — and maybe comes to the conclusion there's not much to regret."

She gazed at me, wide-eyed. "What a horrible thing to say!"

"You asked me. I'm probably wrong."

As soon as we reached the highway I began to keep my eyes open for a black pick-up. No sign of one. So I'm a writer, I imagine things — but it hadn't been imagination last night.

I was waiting for an account of their interview, looking forward to hearing a young, clear-sighted opinion, wondering what they could have found to discuss, even in a mere forty minutes; but it never came — the first time I'd known her to be inarticulate. Perhaps aware of the deficiency, she suddenly said, "At school, in English, they make us stand up and talk for two minutes — you know, on some crappy subject Miss Tennant takes out of a box. Two minutes is forever."

Two minutes is forever, and forty minutes can be an eternity. It was a terrible indictment; once again I felt great pity for Hartman, but with it came that same irritation: however frail he might be he had unlimited money at his disposal — surely there were a thousand things he could be *doing*? And yet, if the wellspring of curiosity, energy, enterprise has dried up in you . . . I asked, "And did you . . . ? What was the expression you used? It was a good one. Did you feel his genes in you?"

"Not a thing. I guess I was crazy to say that — romantic and crazy." The dismissive tone was what I'd hoped to hear: a first indication that Ruth had been right. The girl had expected her real father to mean so much, the meeting would offer some kind of revelation. But the reality had not lived up to the dream; it had been a 'shattering disappointment'. Poor Marisa. I would have found it tragic if it hadn't also opened the escape hatch. Her quest was over; she would now raise no objection to her mother taking her home — home and out of danger.

I felt an urge to cheer her up, and perhaps remove the negative spell which that man and that overwhelming, dazzling house seemed to cast on everyone who entered it. I said, "It's still early. What would you like to do? Something different." On our way through Seaside she had noticed the so-called 'Surreys', on which frantically pedaling tourists plague the local drivers all summer long. If she'd liked I would have paid the astronomical fee and accompanied her on such a ride; but she replied, "Let's pick up Nick and go see your boat. He's crazy about boats."

"Sounds as if you're not."

"They kind of scare me, like horses, but I want to see yours, it sounds fun."

When we got back to the apartment, Ruth had gone to a beauty parlor to do whatever it is that already beautiful women do in beauty parlors. I left a note for her; then drove the two youngsters over to Greg Johansen's marina on the Skipanon. *Mary Celeste* made Nick and Marisa laugh, but they liked her on sight, and of course Nick immediately wanted to cast off and go for a potter. My ready agreement was two-faced, because I knew that after being ignored for a good two weeks the stubborn little diesel would refuse to start. Needless to say the damned thing started at once. So then I had no option but to go sailing.

The morning's fog had cleared completely, leaving good visibility under a sky of uniform grey cloud. I thought we'd voyage the mile and a half to the mouth of the Skipanon and take a cautious look at the great Columbia. We found that the tide was on the ebb, for once cooperating with the river's current, swollen by recent rain; this meant that the whole seething mass of water was moving at maximum speed. We saw a couple of tree trunks, either of which would have smashed *Mary Celeste* to matchsticks, go careering by like speedboats. In spite of this, and in spite of Marisa's very evident uneasiness, Nick was all for voyaging further; but when he saw that the ebb tide and the river's momentum were meeting the Pacific breakers in a head-on collision, hurling fountains of spray a good fifteen or twenty feet into the air, his seafaring ardor went off the boil. On that particular day, and in that kind of weather, I confess my ardor wasn't even lukewarm.

As we retreated up the Skipanon I glanced at Marisa; she looked uncertain and unhappy, and Cross-eye was again peeping from her closed fist. Perhaps the water scared her more than she'd been willing to admit, and she'd agreed to our voyage only to please her best friend. As soon as we touched dry land she scrambled ashore and wandered away on her own.

Noticing Nick's worried frown, I said, "She'll get over it."

"What's the problem?"

"Bio-Father wasn't a big success."

"Yeah, I figured that might happen. She always hopes for too much."

It was only because I was looking at Marisa's retreating back that I noticed the man who was leaning against Greg's boat shed watching us: it had to be us, there was no one else around. My nerves and/or my imagination must have been more on edge than I'd supposed, because I immediately looked for the black pick-up. At the same moment the man, who was young, clean-shaven, unremarkable, turned, sauntered over to a brand-new blue Honda Accord, got into it and drove away; as he did so he passed within a few feet of Marisa, looking her over with frank curiosity; of course, any young man can show that kind of interest in an attractive girl, but by then I felt pretty sure he wasn't just any young man.

So, while Nick and I tucked *Mary Celeste* into her berth, I faced the now-obvious fact that we were being methodically scrutinized, and by people who didn't greatly care whether we knew it or not. It was equally obvious that only the Hartmans, meaning Mark Lindsey, could have instituted the scrutiny — who else? The question was, why? It was hard to read those alien minds, but presumably it was because of the same fear which had made them overreact several times before. Since I was now confident that Marisa wouldn't be staying in Oregon much longer, the implicit threat was less alarming than it would have been, for instance, yesterday. I felt uneasy but no more than that, and I made up my mind not to mention these watchers to the others, not even to Ruth.

When we'd made *Mary Celeste* comfortable, we went in search of Marisa and found her deep in thought, kicking aimlessly at weeds. Nick gave her a searching look, but perhaps knew from experience when to keep quiet; and for the only time since I'd known her, Marisa made no attempt to take part in our conversation as we drove back into Astoria. She didn't even join us in Safeway, even though she usually enjoys shopping and is certainly better at it than either Nick or I. Anyway, we bought enough standard necessities to restock the refrigerator, solving at least one of my practical problems as a host.

As soon as we entered the apartment I realized that something disagreeable had happened. Like all fundamentally straightforward people, Ruth can't really hide her true feelings; she had obviously been waiting on tenterhooks for our return. I waited until Marisa and Nick were busy unpacking the groceries, then maneuvered her out of the kitchen. She immediately said, "Better come to my room, Will. We have to talk." She had spoken softly but Marisa heard. No doubt she had sensed her mother's tension long before I did. She broke her interminable silence and suddenly said, in a strange, high little voice, "If it's about the money, don't bother — he told me."

This took a moment or two to sink in. Ruth said, "He *told* you! What, Marisa?"

"Oh for God's sake! About his damn

will, about changing it." With which she burst into tears and stumbled into her mother's arms, while Nick and I stared open-mouthed.

2

So that explained her unwillingness to talk about their meeting; she had been inarticulate because he'd dumped this weight onto her, and had moreover told her to say nothing about it. I suppose it also explained his own exhaustion, his strange impatience to see the back of us. He had taken an irremediable step, perhaps the first positive step in all those years of self-imposed exile, and he had probably shocked himself in the process.

That he'd come to such a decision was no surprise to Ruth or me — wasn't it what we'd been afraid of? But how stupid my wishful thoughts now seemed, the ones I'd dreamed up while driving Marisa back to Astoria. It had suited me very well to believe that her mood and her silence were caused by disappointment; it was convenient, it tidied things up. Wouldn't you think that in forty-three years I might have learned that nothing in life is ever convenient and nothing ever tidy.

But what a harsh and terrible thing to do to an inexperienced young girl — I refused to believe that the surface sophistication of seventeen had in any way fooled him. It almost seemed like outright cruelty. Yesterday I had thought to myself that he wasn't a man who would pay much attention to other people's feelings; now, in an extension of that thought, I suddenly realized that he could have been motivated by something far worse than cruelty, which is at least personal. Possibly he hadn't been thinking of Marisa at all, had never even comprehended her as a person. The idea of doing what he'd now elected to do might have entered his mind as soon as Ruth told him of the girl's existence — hence the doom-laden parting remark — but the more I thought about it the more likely it seemed that the gun had been loaded long ago, loaded and even aimed. At the very most Marisa would then have been no more than the gentle pressure on the trigger which the instructor is always advising; and the saddest thought of all, considering the mayhem which was now going to ensue, was that she had come so far, with such high hopes, merely to serve this destructive purpose.

Her tears didn't last long; they were only caused by the strain of that secrecy which he had so crassly imposed on her. What little she had to recount only strengthened my suspicions. He'd been weird, he hadn't seemed to know what to say. At first he had just sat there, smiling at her; and then, suddenly: "I'm sorry about what happened to your friend yesterday. The police, all that stupidity. The world is full of hopeless people. Will you apologize to him for me?"

"Yes, I will."

He seemed to have lost himself again, silenced by the impossibility of making what was, to him, meaningless conversation. He had one thing to say but it couldn't be said immediately; so he asked her if she liked the house.

"Oh yes," replied the well-brought-up child, "it's nice." She found it as strange and overwhelming as she found him. "Then he . . . I don't know, I think he asked me about school and how was I getting on, and was I any good at math, and I said no, I hated it. But somehow . . . he wasn't really there at all. He was like that ventriloquist's thing, like that dummy."

I knew what she meant. A hand inside him pulled strings and he moved, talked — jerkily.

Then, out of the blue, he'd said, "Marisa, I was very happy when your mother told me about you." This threw her completely; she thought he must have known about her all along, had no idea Ruth had kept her a secret; it was about the only thing her mother had

240

forgotten to say in briefing her, so she thought he was referring to something which had happened seventeen years before, not yesterday.

Apparently he had heaved himself to his feet — she couldn't watch while he was doing it, terrified he'd fall — and had gone to the nearest window. (Did he, I wondered, spend the greater part of his meaningless life at those windows, looking out over the grim ocean, either visible or invisible? Or did he not even see it as, in another sense, he didn't see his daughter?) After a time, a very long time it seemed to Marisa, he said, "I want this to be a secret between us. Can you keep a secret?"

"Sure."

"I'm a very rich man; maybe you don't know that."

"Well . . . I saw that huge house in Portland, is that yours?"

"Yes, it's mine."

"And now this one."

"When I die . . . I'm going to make

241

you my heir, Marisa; I'm going to leave you a great deal, a very great deal, of money." He turned then and looked at her, and she stared at him, transfixed. She wondered whether he was perhaps insane, and we hadn't warned her. No, we'd have warned her for sure, unless we maybe didn't even know. He said, "Do you understand?"

"I . . . Well, no, not really. I mean . . ."

"You'll be a millionairess, a multi-millionairess."

"But haven't you . . . ? I mean, your family."

"You and Ruth are my family; I have no other."

Hearing this, Ruth looked away, closing her eyes for a moment. I knew she was remembering the intuition which had warned her from the beginning that no good would come of this meeting between father and daughter.

Bravely, in my opinion, Marisa had managed to say to him, "It's . . . very kind of you, but . . . I don't think I want it."

Her bravery was ignored, naturally; perhaps he never even heard her. If you live alone with your thoughts for a long time they become more real than real people. He said, "It'll take a lot of arranging, but that's what attorneys are for." He never asked her how she felt about his intention of turning her life inside out and upside down; never questioned her single comment, that she didn't want to inherit his money. The course was charted, the wheel was lashed and all sails set; if he saw the rocks lying dead ahead he ignored them or, worse, enjoyed the danger they represented.

After he'd once again sent Clemente in search of me, all he said to Marisa was, "Remember, not a word to anyone, not even your mother. They'll know soon enough." No wonder the poor child was relieved to see me; it says a great deal for her strength of mind that not only had she kept his secret but had managed to behave in a reasonable, if uncharacteristic, manner until the moment of bursting into tears; and by then she'd guessed, from her mother's face and her desire to talk to me in private, that the cat was out of the bag anyway.

Ruth's reason for wanting this conversation was that Scott Hartman's principal attorney, Wesley Ryder, had called her about a half-hour after getting the news of his wealthy client's intention; no doubt he'd been shattered and needed time, perhaps aided by a shot of bourbon, to pull himself together. Of course he knew all about the chasm dividing husband and wife; there wasn't much about the Hartmans he didn't know after forty or so years of being their legal adviser. It was he who had persuaded Scott Hartman against divorce seventeen years before. He had held things together (often, as it were, with odd pieces of string and adhesive tape) during the ensuing eight years when the man had spent all his time elsewhere, often abroad, anywhere as long as it wasn't near Christina. After that, following the automobile accident and his principal's total withdrawal from life, he had been forced to deal with Mark Lindsey, finding him as dislikeable as everyone else did, mother-in-law excepted.

None of this made his present predicament any easier, rather the reverse; but like a good lawyer he knew that the first thing he must do was obtain an overall picture, and that his first step in that direction had better be a talk with Ruth; he had called while Marisa and Nick and I were gazing at the Columbia in full spate. Luckily she'd had the presence of mind to press the 'Record' button on the answering machine.

" . . . Ryder, we met many years ago."

"Yes." A rather uncertain voice. "How . . . did you know where to find me?"

"I've just had a call from Scott

Hartman at Hawk Rock. He told me."

"I see."

"He also told me that he wants to change his will."

"Oh my God!" An instinctive reaction.

"I beg your pardon."

"Nothing. Go on."

"To change his will and leave, ah . . . the majority of his estate to your daughter, Miss Marisa Adams. Have I got the name right?"

"Yes. We . . . I so very much hoped this wasn't going to happen."

A telling pause while the legal mind rearranged itself, possibly made a note.

"You imply you suspected it might happen."

"Yes. Yesterday afternoon when I . . . I told him about my daughter. He mentioned changing his will, almost as a joke. We thought, hoped, it might be a joke."

"We? Your daughter and yourself?"

"No, my brother-in-law, Will Adams, and myself."

"Mrs Adams, am I reading you

246

correctly? Are you saying that you only told Mr Hartman that your daughter was his child yesterday afternoon? For the first time?"

"Correct."

"You mean, before that . . . "

"He knew nothing, not even that I was pregnant. If he had known I think he'd have told you."

"Yes, he probably would." Another pause while the legal mind was again rearranged; they try never to show surprise, and are not always successful. "Mrs Adams, certain people are going to conclude that you, ah, influenced Mr Hartman to change his will."

"Mr Ryder, certain people can conclude what they like." She was properly in control of herself now. "For your own information, I never influenced him in any way. Why would I? The last thing I want him to do is change it."

"As you must know, it's a considerable estate. Your daughter would find herself in an entirely new lifestyle."

"My daughter's lifestyle is quite OK as it is. My husband's no multi-millionaire, but he's a successful film director."

"Oh. That Adams."

"He makes more than enough for our small family to live on."

"In fact you're saying you don't want your daughter to inherit this fortune."

"Exactly. That kind of money . . . In my opinion it's dangerous, people can't cope with it. The Hartman family itself is a good example of what I mean. Isn't it?"

"I understand you."

"Then please understand this too, Mr Ryder. I want you to do everything in your power to stop Mr Hartman making this ridiculous move. I want none of it. I won't allow him to wreck my family the way he's . . . No, that's not fair . . . the way he and his wife have wrecked theirs."

A pause. The legal mind getting to grips with reality, which naturally made the legal voice sound less sure of itself:

an effect reality has on the best of us. "I'm sure I don't have to tell you, he doesn't like people trying to change his mind for him."

"You changed it before. When he wanted a divorce."

"You remember that."

"Of course. There's nothing I don't remember about . . . that time."

"Understandable, I guess."

"And he hasn't made up his mind about this. He only began to consider it yesterday — as I told you."

"I think some such course may have occurred to him before. More than once."

"Maybe. She's an impossible woman, and his daughter . . . I'm sure she's nice enough, but he doesn't seem to like her very much."

Silence. We do not perjure ourselves.

"What I'm saying is that I believe you and I, working together, can make him reconsider — and then change his mind."

"And what I'm saying is, it won't

be easy. You saw him yesterday, you know what I'm talking about."

"The impossible will take a little longer."

"I'm sorry?"

"I was quoting. Who from, I can't remember."

"Very well, Mrs Adams. I think I know where I stand as far as you're concerned. Thank you for being, ah, so frank. We'll doubtless be meeting within the next few days."

"The sooner the better. I want to take my daughter home; she should be back in school."

Ruth first played me this recording when we were finally alone together, Nick having taken Marisa, washed and combed, cold water on the eyes, for a hamburger. I felt we were all in this together, would sink or swim together, so at my suggestion she played it a second time when they returned. Marisa listened to it gravely. At the end she said, "Wow, you were great, Mom. Talk about cool!"

"Cool was not what I felt."

"I bet Dad . . . Jack's right. I bet you were quite an actress." Then, glancing away, frowning, "I don't know. I mean, why didn't you tell him? Then — before I was born."

Nick said, "Come on, that's obvious. No tell, no pressure."

Marisa looked at her mother with raised brows. Ruth added, "No pressure, no blackmail."

"Oh God, as if you would!"

"You haven't," said Ruth dryly, "met Christina Hartman. I pray you never do. Blackmail will be the first thing she'll think of."

An hour later, Wesley Ryder's office called to say that Mr Ryder had made an appointment to meet with Mr Hartman at eleven next morning. Would Mrs and Miss Adams and Mr Will Adams be able to attend? With a sinking heart I replied that we would.

Of all the awkward situations in which I'd been involved from time to time, none had ever possessed the clinging, adhesive quality of this one; it was like trying to shake from one's fingers a piece of some irritating plastic wrap. Not too long ago I'd been confidently telling myself that Marisa could be taken home, a thousand miles away from the storm which was obviously about to break; now Scott Hartman's manic selfishness, his total disregard for anyone else, was bringing the inexorable legal system into play: a time waster without parallel. I wondered whether Ruth would have the courage (she might well call it cowardice) to turn her back on the law and Mr Hartman, and take her daughter back to LA regardless.

Even this recourse, I then realized, was about to be defeated by, of all people, my brother Jack, who was intending to come up to Oregon at the weekend. If things at Hawk Rock were settled by tomorrow evening his arrival might prove providential in that he could take Ruth and Marisa home with him; if things were held up or went wrong — more likely — he'd inevitably become involved himself. His family was the most important thing in his life, and if it came to a choice he'd kiss any movie goodbye without compunction: a loving gesture which, in the case of this particular movie, might well prove to be a career breaker.

When we called him he said he intended to arrive the day after tomorrow, Saturday, possibly around noon — there was a connecting flight, Portland-Astoria, so nobody need drive up to collect him. In reply to the usual terse questioning, Ruth told him that, yes, Marisa had met Hartman, and hadn't been impressed; had, in fact, been bitterly disappointed. It was over; it was done with.

His answer made her grimace; she handed the phone to me. "Will, what's going on? She's holding out on me again."

"Of course she isn't."

"This guy, there aren't . . . complications?"

I cursed the symbiosis which binds people who care for one another, but the question called for a quick, firm lie: "None, Jack. He's in pretty bad shape, smashed himself up in a car, permanent cripple. We have to treat him gently."

"And Marisa took him in her stride?"

"As Ruth said, he was a huge disappointment."

I seemed to have calmed him — not the effect I usually have on my brother. He said, "I'm damn glad you're there, Will. Look after them."

"Of course. And don't worry, we're out of the wood. There's nothing you could do if you were here." I put the phone down. Ruth and I regarded each other. She said, "Out of the wood, eh? With one foot caught! We're not having the best of luck, are we, Will?"

It was true — in spite of the fact that everything had gone our way: Marisa had found her father, and her quest was over; she'd been disappointed in him which, as we'd agreed, was the best thing that could happen; she was even ready to go home. Everything had gone our way, and still the adhesive situation wouldn't allow us to move. Unless . . . I put forward my cowardly suggestion: "I suppose you couldn't just walk out on the whole hideous mess."

"No." As I'd expected. "Scott would be hurt and angry, and then God knows what he'd do. This has to be defeated, squarely, erased from his mind."

"As Wesley Ryder pointed out, he's a man who's not easy to defeat."

"That's how he seems, but Christina defeated him over me, didn't she?"

Yes, I thought, but that game was played seventeen years ago by a different set of rules. What a joker life sometimes is. The expected danger had crept up on us and caught us unawares by taking the unexpected form of Scott Hartman himself. It was his door in which the foot was caught, his trap. Come to think of it, hadn't this always been so, from the moment Jack and

Ruth had told Marisa, over the eggs Benedict, that Jack wasn't her father?

3

We left Nick in Astoria; he had a date with the Maritime Museum, one of the town's few outstanding diversions which would keep him happy for hours. It was good to see someone of his age so perfectly self-contained, so able to amuse himself without resorting to the mindlessness of television.

At the mouth of the Columbia it was a grey drizzling day, but only twenty miles to the south, around Arch Cape, the sun was breaking through and the last tatters of morning mist were trailing up the pine-covered slopes, dissolving into a brilliant blue sky. As we climbed the hills towards Hawk Rock we could see a great barrier of cloud reclining on the ocean along the entire western horizon, not generally a happy portent. We hadn't spoken much on the journey. Ruth's determined expression indicated that she was arming herself for conflict. From time to time I caught a glimpse of Marisa in the rear mirror. She looked apprehensive, as well she might, also a touch mutinous; I put the latter down to the fact that Ruth had made her wear a dress. The only dresses you see in our neck of the woods are worn by businesswomen, all the others squeeze themselves into pants — even those whose posteriors are as wide as their overall height; Marisa made a pleasant change, even if she didn't think so.

As Clemente led us up all those white stairs to the bridge of the liner I said, hoping to cheer her up a little, "You've brought your cross-eyed toad, haven't you?"

It did produce a smile. "Of course." She was already holding him in the pocket of her dress.

"Good. Something tells me we're going to need all the luck we can get."

We found Scott Hartman in that huge V-shaped room, talking to a spare balding man who wore old-fashioned steel-rimmed glasses low on his long thin nose. This wasn't the attorney, Wesley Ryder, who had the kind of plump voice which could never emanate from a thin body. I think we were taken aback — I know I was — to be introduced to Karel Reinmann, one of the world's leading neurologists. I remembered that he now lived and worked in San Francisco, but San Francisco was five hundred miles away, and he was not a man who would come running when big money raised a finger. I could only suppose that he'd been one of the many surgeons and doctors, all eminent I'm sure, who had put Hartman together again after his accident. The fact that he'd been visiting Hawk Rock disturbed me, not from any medical point of view but because his presence added a new dimension to Hartman himself, Hartman as opponent. He was about to take an important legal step; his body had been smashed in an accident; had there been mental problems connected with that accident? If so, what was more natural at this moment than a desire to make sure all was well, and who more natural to give that assurance than his old specialist? I'd imagined we were up against a rich man's whim. We weren't — we were up against his organized determination. Yes, that was disturbing all right.

I think Ruth may have been thinking along the same lines. Our eyes met for a second before we turned to say goodbye to Dr Reinmann who was just leaving for Portland airport; he left in a Volvo station wagon, chauffeur-driven. Apart from Clemente and his wife, how many other people were hidden away in the working parts of this ménage?

Hartman himself was no more reassuring; he was less awkward than before, the lassitude we'd all known replaced by febrile nervous energy, color burning on the cheekbones above the almost skeletal hollows of his face. Decision seemed to have brought the invalid back to life, and I could see that Ruth was unsure of how best to say, to this changed man, the things she was determined to say; her natural straightforwardness gave her little leeway in any case: "Scott, before the lawyer arrives, may I ask you — please, please reconsider this thing."

He laughed, a soft, brittle sound. "Dear Ruth, you must be the only person around who's not after my money." And he looked at her so searchingly and with such sudden gentleness that for the first time I had an inkling of the feeling which had once bound them together. "But then you never were after it."

"No, never. And I'm not taking it now."

"I'm not giving it to you, my dear, I'm giving it to . . . our daughter."

Ruth glanced at Marisa who said, "I don't want it either."

He transferred the gentle look to her and shook his head, staring. "What a heartbreaker you're going to be, Marisa. You look lovely today."

Unwillingly perhaps, she replied, "I guess it's the dress."

But Ruth was not going to be deflected; she tried again: "You're evading the issue, Scott."

"I've always been good at that, it's a rich man's device." Yes indeed, he had changed almost out of recognition; for a moment I wondered whether the change was natural or perhaps — and perhaps under Karel Reinmann's supervision — chemically induced. It didn't matter; either way it made him formidable.

He said to Marisa, "Of course you don't want the money — only grasping people *want* that kind of money." No doubt about the objects of the reference. "But when you're older . . . I assure you it'll be a comfort to know it's there."

Ruth gave a wry smile. "Oh, Scott, do we have to fight you every inch of the way?"

"No, you can just surrender and let me win; it'll be much easier. I'm a spoiled child from way back; I'm used to winning."

The deafening rattle of a helicopter suddenly burst over us as it cleared the crest of Hawk Rock. Hartman said, "Good. Here's Wesley."

In my wanderings while other people talked I had seen, on the far side of the house near the big swimming pool, what I'd thought to be tennis courts which had never been completed; the helicopter, having wheeled out over the ocean to lose height, now clattered in to make its landing there. A few minutes later Wesley Ryder joined us, smoothing his white hair, ruffled by the rotor which had now clacked to a standstill. I'd expected him to be plump, and he was; the smooth pink face, with a small cherubic mouth and bright, pale blue eyes, must have been a considerable help in his legal career; it never does an attorney any harm to look harmless, even infantile. He almost bowed over Ruth's hand. "Mrs Adams, nice to see you again — you haven't changed at all. And this is Marisa. And you must be the brother-in-law — glad you could be with us, Will." And, turning: "Scott, my dear boy, you're looking great. Great." Having got all this out of the way in record time and with nerve-wracking aplomb, he stood there rubbing his fat little hands together and beaming at us. The performance seemed to have irritated Ruth; her voice was sharp: "I've asked Scott to give up this idea. He's refused."

"And that," said Hartman, "is the present state of play. Now let's get on with it."

The attorney stopped rubbing his hands together and sighed; then pinched his nose between forefinger and thumb. "It's not for me to lay down the law, Scott, but — "

"You usually do."

"As an old friend, not as a lawyer. I was going to say 'friend of the family' but that may not be in order."

"It isn't."

"Then as *your* old friend, I'm going to ask you to think again."

"Wesley, the idea didn't come to me yesterday, on the spur of the moment."

I must have reacted to this in some small way because he glanced at me. I'd been sure from the start that the idea hadn't come to him seriously yesterday, when he'd met Marisa for the first time, and certainly not on the spur of the moment, but I hadn't expected the man himself to confirm my suspicion; his attorney had felt the same way — hadn't he said to Ruth on the phone, "I think some such course may have occurred to him before, more than once." I felt a stirring of anger: how blindly selfish can anyone be? He wasn't considering Ruth, whom he had once loved, he wasn't considering Marisa, the result of that love, and he wasn't considering his old friend and lawyer who had, I was sure, served him honorably and well for so many years.

He was considering only himself: "I'm a spoiled child from way back, I'm used to winning." Perhaps it was just as well that none of it was my business and I therefore had to keep quiet.

I was surprised at the steel in Ruth's voice when she suddenly said, "Scott, I've no reason to like your wife, you know that, but all this about the money — it's nothing to do with Marisa or me; you're attacking Christina, and probably your son-in-law as well. And it's not . . . it's not worthy of you; you're a bigger person than that."

I've never thought honesty to be the best policy, nor even a mildly wise one, but perhaps because she herself is incapable of dishonesty what she'd said struck home; for a second or two he even looked ashamed of himself. She added, "I don't like Marisa being used as a . . . a machine gun in your family war, and I don't like being used myself."

"That's not what I'm doing."

"Of course it's what you're doing. So

I'm going to say it again, and this time in front of Mr Ryder — I don't want your money, and Marisa doesn't want it either."

"I haven't heard her say so."

"But you have, I said it just now." She was flushed and her voice had risen into another key. "Mother's right — the money's nothing to do with me, it scares me."

Wesley Ryder spread both pink hands. "And even that," he said, "isn't enough for you?"

"No, it's irrelevant."

I think this was probably the most barefacedly selfish remark I've ever heard anyone make. I felt another heave of anger in my stomach. Since I couldn't speak I would greatly have preferred not to be in the room at all, but Ruth had insisted on my presence, and for her sake I'd stay; if anything was irrelevant it was me.

Patiently the attorney was now saying, "And Scott, there are many other things to be considered. I don't think you've any idea of the havoc this would cause in your estate, let alone the financial loss. I won't speak in human terms, Mrs Adams has just done that most eloquently, but I can certainly speak in terms of the whole enormous portfolio — finely adjusted investments, trusts, debentures which — "

The man who was used to winning cut him short as if with a whip: "Wesley, for some forty years I've been paying you large sums to handle those matters for me. I'm glad they're finely adjusted, they should be. But they can't have occupied a fiftieth of your time — they're on automatic pilot. What I'm saying is, you owe me, Wesley — your office owes me thousands of hours of work, and now I want that work done, and quickly."

Elderly and respected lawyers don't like having words like these thrown in their faces, least of all in front of strangers. Obviously Wesley Ryder was only prepared to take it because of the extent of the Hartman wealth.

His natural reaction was anger — a little pulse began to throb at the side of his jaw — but he contained the anger and said, with dignity, it seemed to me, "I've always thought you were satisfied with my firm's work."

"I am. But I'm not listening to a lot of crap about investments and debentures. As far as I'm concerned the whole damn thing can stay the way it is. I'm demanding that the money generated be channeled in a different direction. I therefore want to change my will — doesn't that make sense?"

"It's an oversimplification."

"You're the lawyer, it's up to you to desimplify it; that's how you guys get rich."

Obviously we were being given a glimpse of the autocratic, impatient, perhaps impossible man Scott Hartman had once been before violent physical injury had notched him down and kicked the shit out of him. But when I studied his face more closely I could see that all this argument was taking its toll; it had become rigid and pale, and I think he was having to exert great willpower and energy to subdue some form of shaking, not unlike that particular symptom of Alzheimer's. Impossible or not, selfish and arrogant or not, I found that in spite of myself he commanded my respect; I had to admire his tenacity even though I didn't agree with its objectives.

I suppose the sight of a man rebelling against the power of circumstance and fate, which had already dealt him such a crushing blow, calls out to the courage, or lack of it, in other men. And perhaps in women too, because I could see that even Ruth's expression had softened as she looked at him; not, I knew, that she would for one moment relinquish the stand she'd taken against him, but perhaps something in him at that moment reminded her of the man with whom she'd once been so helplessly in love. Marisa simply gazed at him with wide, startled eyes; for a young girl this visit to Hawk Rock was proving to be a crash course in what might be called 'The Inhumanities', and it hadn't yet got into its stride.

As for Wesley Ryder, he pursed his baby lips, then said, "I think perhaps we should reconsider my position, Scott. I represent *you* and always have, but in recent years I've been forced into . . . an affiliation with other members of your family. There may be a conflict of . . . not of interest and not of loyalty but, ah . . . " He waved a plump hand and finished, lamely for him, "A conflict."

Hartman snorted and lay back in his chair, silent. Then he said, "If my old friend and I are going to reconsider his position — which I assure you, Wesley, we're not — it had better be done in private. Ruth, I know you won't mind. And Marisa, and Will . . . " He reached out and pressed a bell push on the table beside him. The Filipino appeared as if by magic.

"Clemente, will you serve coffee to my friends? In the library."

"Sir, if I please may say — "

"Not now. Just coffee in the library."

Perhaps he should have allowed the man to speak; it would certainly have saved his friends from a shock, even if at the same time it might have embarrassed his attorney who had obviously been sworn to silence: because when Clemente opened the library door we realized that the helicopter had transported more than Wesley Ryder to Hawk Rock; from the far end of the brilliant sunlit room Christina Hartman and Mark Lindsey stood staring at us. Hostility, even hatred, personified.

★ ★ ★

After a couple of hours at the Maritime Museum, Nick became aware of his stomach groaning for sustenance; then he recalled that owing to the atmosphere in my apartment that morning, apprehension and more than a suspicion of dread, he hadn't eaten his usual breakfast, making do with a single slice of toast instead of four, and a single cup of coffee instead of two. His experience of Astoria's cafés had not been encouraging, and he decided that what he'd really like would be two thick slices of toast with sharp Cheddar cheese on top, put under the broiler for five or six minutes until it was golden and bubbling, and some French mustard to go with it.

His mouth was watering with expectation by the time he'd trudged up the hill and let himself into the house, using the key I'd given him. However, when he inserted the second key into the door of the apartment it wouldn't turn; he was just thinking to himself that he'd never noticed me having any trouble with it when he realized that the door was not locked. This struck him as odd; if I'd failed to lock it he wouldn't have been surprised, considering the state we were all in when we'd left for Hawk Rock, but he had gone out a good half-hour after us and distinctly remembered making certain it was secure. He opened the door and went in, and was greeted cheerily by a man in white coveralls who was working on the water heater in the kitchen: "Hi! Sorry about the door — kept blowing shut."

He was a very ordinary-looking man of about thirty, with a sickly mustache and sandy hair growing thin on top — but Nick had noticed that many of the youngish males in Astoria sported a sickly mustache and most of them were slightly bald, perhaps because they all wore baseball caps and never took them off, certainly not in a restaurant and possibly not even in bed. He had removed the front from the heater and was tinkering with the works. "Regular service," he said by way of explanation. "Mr Adams must have forgotten. Caretaker let me in."

Nick says he can't remember exactly when he began to think this man was a phony. He knew that any service person entering an empty dwelling usually left the door open: to advertise his presence and reassure anyone who cared that he wasn't stealing the CD player; so the door had kept blowing shut, and it would be normal to mention the fact. But Nick didn't think it likely I'd forget the man was coming, and here again he was led back to the tense circumstances of the morning, aggravated by the ongoing argument between Ruth and her daughter as to whether or not Marisa should wear a dress. For reassurance he went to my desk and looked in my diary; the water heater wasn't mentioned, only the fact that at eight the following morning I was due to take my car in for a service. So, Nick told himself, if I hadn't made a note of the appointment I might well have forgotten all about it.

He also told himself he was being oversuspicious anyway, and he knew why: because of his experiences yesterday with the blockhouse guards, Mark Lindsey, and finally the police. In Thank God It's Friday he had made light of the whole incident, not wishing us to think him fussy and self-important; but he had admitted to himself that he'd made a pretty good balls of the operation, shouldn't have been caught with his pants down in the first place; and he couldn't get out of his mind Mark Lindsey's face, which he had seen more clearly, in many senses, than the rest of us; it kept reappearing, hard-eyed and callous, a brutal kind of face — and he really wouldn't have been surprised if Lindsey had pulled out a fingernail or two in order to speed the interrogation.

His hunger had become demanding, but he wasn't about to prepare his cheese toast within a few feet of the suspect stranger. He retired to the junk room and sat on his bed. Hadn't I said of his arrest, "It was a warning, and a heavy warning too." This had seemed to him to make sense. Indeed, from the moment of my saying it he'd been wondering if the warning might lead to something else. Like what? Like this guy in the kitchen.

(Of course it's clear to me, *now*, that I should have told him about the man who had been watching the house, about the black pick-up which had followed us along the coast highway, about the other watching man at Greg's marina.)

Again Mark Lindsey's face was thrust close to his own and the hard voice rasped, "Don't fuck with me. Know a lady called Adams, Mrs Ruth Adams?"

It now struck him as odd that the man had arrived to service the heater at a time when everyone was absent. It almost looked as if the time had been chosen *because* Will Adams, who rented the apartment, was out and would be tied up with a complicated meeting all day. If this premise was correct, and if the heating man was really up to no good, he would have been advised by someone who knew about the meeting — someone like . . . Oh God, here he came again . . . like Mark Lindsey.

Poor Nick! Because he's big for his age, and intelligent, one tends to forget that he's only seventeen, and as unsure of himself as any other seventeen-year-old. Like Marisa, he was balanced on the seesaw between being a child and becoming an adult; and if he was inclined to dwell on his arrest it was a very normal reaction; being accused of 'substance abuse' is the kind of thing which is apt to stand out in the mind of a teenager who has never touched drugs.

Something else occurred to him; he sat and thought about it for a while, and then returned to the kitchen to verify the thought. The man had just finished replacing the front cover of the heater, the job was evidently over; but as he tossed a screwdriver into his tool box, open on the floor beside him, Nick was able to take a good look inside it. Yes, he'd been right. His father, like an ordinary practical American, wasn't about to call an engineer every time any little thing went wrong in his house — he fixed it himself; and not three months ago he had fixed the water heater in the utility room. His father was an automobile mechanic and possessed many tools, but none he had used on the heater were as small and precise as some of the ones Nick glimpsed inside this box just before the man folded it shut. Had he shut it because he'd noticed Nick's interest? Or did some water heaters require small, finicky tools? Open question.

The man now tidied up after himself like a good workman, threw away the bits and pieces, picked up the tool box and said, "OK. That'll see you through for another year." As he turned out of the kitchen he added, "We mail the bill. I guess Mr Adams sends it to his landlord, most renters do. Have a nice one." And he went across the living room and out through the front door.

Nick waited a moment; then followed. From the hall window, the one I'd so carelessly left open on that rainy night, he saw the man emerge from the house, go to a nondescript van, get into it and drive away. After further thought he went downstairs to the ground floor, opened the door leading to the basement, descended another flight and rang Andy Swensen's bell. The Swensens were just sitting down to two steaming bowls of split-pea and ham soup; it smelled so good that Nick's hunger came rampaging back. He said, "Did you let the water-heater guy into Mr Adams' apartment?"

"Sure did," said Andy, returning to the table.

"Recognize him?"

"You kidding? Those guys change jobs every two weeks." He blew on his soup. Mrs Swensen smiled: nice-looking kid. What went on up there? Who was screwing whom?

Nick said, "What time did he come?"

"You with the FBI or somethin'? Came around eleven, eleven-fifteen."

Nick closed the door on them and withdrew. Did it take two hours to service a small water heater? As he again climbed the stairs, he wished he'd asked whether the man had also serviced the other two apartments, in which case two hours . . .

Oh for God's sake! Any more of this, he'd be around the bend. And what did he think the guy was going to *do* in the apartment? Will Adams wasn't even involved with the Hartmans. But, he thought as he at last prepared his cheese toast, Marisa and her mother were involved with the Hartmans, and they were staying in the apartment, weren't they? If something awful happened to Marisa because her best friend, Nick Deering, was too dumb to see what was under his nose . . .

OK, what *was* under his nose? While his cheese was gently broiling, he wandered around examining the place; he didn't know it all that well but everything seemed to be exactly as it always was. Had the guy been bugging the phones? Great idea! What for? Had he put a bomb under Marisa's bed?

Nick, you are nuttier than a fruitcake, you are the world's number one goofball, you are that famous old broad who sees men exposing themselves every which way she turns, you are *certifiable*!

But as he sat down to eat he thought that all those finicky tools really had been a bit weird . . .

★ ★ ★

The easy thing for us to have done, on coming face to face with Christina Hartman and her son-in-law, would have been to turn away and take our coffee elsewhere; but Ruth merely paused for a moment, then smiled at Clemente and went forward.

Mrs Hartman said, "You don't seem surprised to see us."

"Why should I be? Presumably you're here to defend your interests." Before the other woman could find words, she added, "This is my daughter, Marisa." And, putting a hand on the girl's arm, "Mrs Hartman, honey. I think you've already met Mr Lindsey."

His gray, shallow eyes regarded them both without expression; he said, "So that's why she used a phony name." Christina gave her a look of unconcealed hatred, then swung around and showed us her back. She must have known that the vivid light of Hawk Rock was not kind to a woman so well acquainted with the plastic surgeon. In the soft marbled gloom of EastWest Drive there had been no mistaking the remains of unusual beauty. Here, in the glare of those vast windows, with her black sculptured hair, she looked like some savage character out of a No play, blazing eyes staring from a pale mask.

My immediate reaction on seeing Lindsey had been an urge to ask him why we were being watched; but I quickly realized this would achieve nothing. If I wanted to complain I could go to the police, who would take no action — we weren't being harassed, and it's not against the law to observe people. Also I hadn't mentioned the watchers to Ruth and Marisa, and didn't want to scare them now: not at this awkward point of the proceedings.

There was a tap on the door and Clemente appeared with coffee, breaking the tension. Looking around, I was surprised to notice that the library was well stocked; and the books hadn't been bought by the yard either — they were much used. So Hartman didn't only stare out of windows.

As soon as the Filipino had withdrawn, and still with her back to us, Mrs Hartman said, "Didn't take you long to find him, did it?"

"No," replied Ruth, "it was easy. I don't know why you bothered to lie to me."

"I'd have thought that was obvious."

"Damned obvious," added Lindsey. "Since you've induced him to change his will."

Ruth sighed. "I don't want it

changed. As far as I'm concerned your wife's his next of kin and his legal heir, and that's the end of it."

I must say I was surprised at the absence of this wife; perhaps Mark Lindsey sensed it, or perhaps he was used to defending her absences: "Susan couldn't make it today; she has an important meeting."

I gave him an understanding smile. He colored. What meeting, I wondered, could be more important to an heiress than preserving the vast fortune she was in danger of losing? A wedding shower, one of her Vassar buddies? Or did she have an appointment with the manicurist in aid of that *maddening* broken nail? Or, indeed, was she so mindlessly self-assured that she didn't believe the danger was real?

Lindsey guessed from the smile what I was thinking. "My wife isn't great on business."

I said, "I'm sure you're great on doing it for her."

He looked at me with loathing. "I

can't imagine what you're doing here anyway."

"Neither can I, but your father-in-law said he wanted me around." It seemed worth adding, "I'm not sure he wanted you around."

Ruth laid a restraining hand on my arm. "We're all in this together. The least we can do is behave in a reasonably civilized manner."

Christina Hartman gave what was supposed to be a snort of ironical amusement and turned back to face us. "If you call it civilized to go chasing after a man, a sick man, who . . . dispensed with your services more than seventeen years ago . . . "

"That's a lousy thing to say." I think it surprised all of us to hear Marisa's voice, trembling with anger. "Mother didn't come to Oregon to see Mr Hartman, *I* came to see him."

"Oh! Why?"

"I . . . I'd just discovered he was my . . . real father, and I wanted to meet him."

Mrs Hartman said, "Nonsense. She sent you, didn't she?"

"No. She followed me; she wanted to stop me."

The two of them exchanged a look of total disbelief. Lindsey said, "Stop you?"

"Yes," said Ruth. "I was afraid something like this might happen."

Lindsey raised his eyes to heaven. "You honestly expect us to believe that?"

"Not really. Neither of you seem to know the truth when it's staring you in the face."

"The truth!" Christina Hartman came closer, once again demonstrating the cruel dissimilarity between the two women. "The truth is that within twenty-four hours of your finding him he's disowning Susan and leaving me with — "

"We'll take you to court of course." Evidently Lindsey thought it unwise to reveal what she was being left with. "We . . . that is, my wife will fight you with everything she's got. You'll regret you ever started this, Mrs Adams."

I said, "For God's sake, what's the point in fighting Mrs Adams? She agrees with you, hasn't she said so?"

"Haven't we said we don't believe her?"

During this exchange Ruth had busied herself pouring five cups of coffee. I was surprised Christina Hartman had allowed her to do this, since it put Ruth in the position of quasi-hostess while she herself was relegated to a supporting role as guest. Then I noticed her hands; they were shaking so much with rage that she couldn't have managed the coffeepot anyway. She said, "I knew you'd come back — your kind always does. Isn't it enough that you ruined my marriage?"

Ruth's hand didn't even shake as she poured the last cup: "Yes, I was told you were going around saying that. You don't believe it and neither does anyone else."

"What do you know about what

people . . . people who matter believe?"

I said, "Even the people who matter aren't that stupid, Mrs Hartman — your marriage had been on the rocks for many years before Ruth met your husband."

"That's a lie! Mark . . . ?"

I continued before he could utter another inane threat: "What's the matter with you both? Can't you even listen? My sister-in-law's told Mr Hartman over and over again that neither she nor her daughter want a nickel of his money."

Christina Hartman laughed in my face and Mark Lindsey said, "Stop treating us like fools." At which Marisa could contain herself no longer: "Oh, don't bother! Why don't we just take the damn money? It might be fun being millionaires."

It was a shallow, even childish, remark, and therefore out of character; but that was its great strength, that's why it hit those two shallow people where it hurt — she had voiced their own nightmare fears. While they were staring at her in amazed horror, the door opened abruptly and Scott Hartman stood framed in the doorway. I wondered whether his attorney or Clemente had finally broken the news of their presence; his anger was truly alarming to see. Quietly but with stinging venom he said, "I thought I told you two not to come near this house ever again."

Marisa had delivered the straight left, and her father had followed it with a savage right hook, but the effort seemed to have cost him what little strength he possessed; his former élan, and even his color, had deserted him; the loose clothes now seemed to emphasize the scarecrow body and his eyes had receded into their sockets. I think the sight of him, more than his words, stunned his wife and son-in-law, neither of whom had probably seen him for months, perhaps years.

Christina Hartman pulled herself together first — from habit, I supposed, for they must have faced one another a hundred times in this or that impossible situation. She said, "Even Mrs Adams respects our right to be here — to . . . defend our interests."

He looked at Ruth and said, "Mrs Adams is the kindest and gentlest woman on earth — she'd respect the rights of . . . of a gopher undermining her house." And then, voice snapping, "You have no interests to defend, Christina, none."

"Oh, I think so." Mark Lindsey had also recovered. "You're planning to disown my wife — "

"I'm planning nothing of the sort. I shall see that my daughter can continue . . . living the life to which her mother has accustomed her. She'll be provided for, handsomely. I'm not sure she'll want to share it with you, but that's her business."

"Scott," said his wife, "you absolutely cannot do this thing. Think of the scandal."

"What scandal? Nobody will give a

goddamn; they're all tired of us and our scandals. If you weren't a fool, as well as the most selfish woman who ever lived, you'd know it."

Her eyes glittered at these insults; they had probably been voiced before, more than once, but not perhaps in front of other people, and people like us too! She said, "I don't think you understand. We shall be forced to go to court and plead that you're mentally incapable."

"Oh," he said, moving towards her, "is that what you'll be forced to do?"

"You don't expect Mark and Susan to take a thing like this lying down."

"They can take it in any position they choose. And while they're about it they can consider that a grandchild or two might have strengthened their position no end."

"You know perfectly well Susan's much too delicate — "

"Too delicate, my ass! She's too selfish; she's your daughter."

"Insults mean nothing. You know

this'll end up in court. I doubt if you *are* entirely sane anyway."

He nodded, eying her, holding onto the wall for support. "Remember Dr Reinmann, Christina?"

She glanced away as if the name had stung her. "What about him?"

"He stayed here last night."

"Reinmann." Her voice had faded.

"He's just as happy about my state of mind right now as he was last time he appeared in court and made you look such a grasping fool."

"But," began his son-in-law, "wasn't that after your accident, nine — ?"

"Yes, and nine years ago you hadn't met my daughter, so you've no idea what Karel Reinmann can do in a court of law without even raising his voice. If you try to prove I'm too weak in the head to draw up a new will, you're the one he'll commit — and rightly."

"I see," said his wife who had again recovered. "You don't care if this woman is made to testify, dragged through the mud. I'm sure her husband will care; he'll probably divorce her."

Ruth opened her mouth to reply, but he held up a bony hand to prevent her. "What do you mean by that?"

"There's no proof the girl is your child, none at all."

"Of course there's always DNA," added Lindsey unpleasantly, "but I doubt if you're willing to risk it."

"Seventeen years ago!" Christina Hartman laughed. "You're the one who'll look a fool."

Hartman shook his head pityingly. "You're such a liar yourself you can't even understand that some people are truthful. Ruth would never lie to me about Marisa, never." He turned to his lawyer. "You going to tell 'em, Wesley, or shall I?"

Ryder ran a fat little hand over his white hair. He looked very unhappy; perhaps there was a conflict of interest here too. "The fact is, Mrs Hartman, that, ah . . . it makes no difference."

"What do you mean, no difference?

My husband claims the girl is his illegitimate daughter and there's not an atom of proof she's anything of the sort, that's the difference."

Ruth moved closer to Marisa, took the girl's arm and slipped it through her own, hugging it close to her side.

"Mr Hartman," continued Wesley Ryder manfully, "can leave his estate to Miss Adams, if that's what he decides to do, whether she's his daughter or not."

"And that," added his client, "will include my three houses and everything in them." I thought of Gainsborough and Bonnard and Manet, and heaven knew what treasures in rooms we'd never seen. And where, I wondered, was the third house?

Christina Hartman's mouth opened; and closed again. She looked at Mark Lindsey.

"For God's sake," snapped her husband, "let's not make a production of it. It's my money, they're my houses. I can leave them to Clemente if I want — or to the cats' home. Correct, Wesley?"

"Ah . . . correct."

"We'd contest it." Lindsey had cast away the smooth mask; without it he looked ugly and dangerous, and another five years older. "Susan would contest the will."

"I guess she could," replied his father-in-law thoughtfully. "That kind of thing's darned expensive, but the sum I intend to give her would cover it. Wouldn't leave you much to live on, but you're a talented young businessman, you can always make money, can't you?"

This was a jibe, a barbed one, and there was some personal resonance in it. I wondered if, in the past, his father-in-law might have had to rescue him from a disastrous financial predicament; the younger man's angry and defensive expression seemed to corroborate the suspicion — he wasn't good at hiding what he felt.

Hartman smiled. "By all means try

it. I'll be dead of course, but you'll see my ghost gibbering at the judge's elbow. You contesting *my* will — I wouldn't miss that for anything." The smile broadened into a grin which, on that ruined face, was disturbing.

It was wrong, indeed utterly amoral, that he should be enjoying himself under such excruciating circumstances, and I was just wondering why I could so easily excuse him, when he gave the answer to my thought as neatly as if he'd read it. Not smiling any more, but as grim as the reaper he somewhat resembled, he said, "In the last . . . oh God, forty years, I've been happy once. Once. And that was when I was in love with this beautiful woman here — and between us we made that beautiful child." He smiled at Ruth and Marisa, an exhausted shadow of a smile; then ran a hand over his face and wiped it away. "I'm tired, I must rest, and I mean right now."

He staggered a little as he turned towards the door. His wife, face working with rage, said, "Jesus! What a cruel man you are."

"Cruel?" He looked back at her, one hand on the doorpost for balance. "You cheated me out of marrying the girl I loved."

She turned away from us all and stood looking out of one of those glaring windows.

"Good, you haven't forgotten. Then you wrecked the happiness I had with Ruth. If you'd done any of it for love I could have understood. But you don't do things for love, only for money. Now I'm cruel because I'm taking the money away. As ye sow, Christina."

I noticed that fear seemed to have melted Mark Lindsey as if he were a wax figurine, melted him and remolded him into another, more brutish, shape — his real shape perhaps (Nick would instantly have recognized it). He took a shambling pace after his father-in-law. "Is this your last word? You're really going to do it?"

"My God," muttered Hartman, again

moving away. "I've been saying so for nearly four hours. Yes, I'm going to do it. If any of you want anything . . . food, drink, anything, ask Clemente." He was out of the door now, voice diminishing. "He's a wonderful guy — I bet he can even rustle up some cyanide." Laughter, like a consumptive's cough, and he was gone.

His departure left a vibrating silence behind it. A blue jay shrieked somewhere outside among the trees, and in this situation the mocking, laughter-like cry had ironical overtones. Mark Lindsey was staring at Ruth and Marisa, his face expressionless. If he had given them a glare of undisguised hatred it would, oddly enough, have been less malevolent. The blank stare negated them — they were beneath his contempt. This, I thought, is what he is, and mere words are only part of his mask. Then he turned back to his mother-in-law and Wesley Ryder, saying, "We can do without your services, Wesley. You're a dead loss."

"You must remember, I was Scott's attorney long before — "

"Save your breath. We'll be using someone else." I thought to myself that the return journey in the helicopter would be a silent one.

Christina Hartman looked from one man to the other. Her age was showing; she even seemed at a loss. "No," she said, "I can't do without Wesley; he's got to advise me about — "

"Oh for God's sake! He's screwing us." Possibly she'd never heard her son-in-law so savage; possibly she didn't know him at all. But Ryder was no weakling; he turned to Ruth: "We shall have to reconsider, Mrs Adams. I take it you still want to stop Scott doing this."

"Yes, of course."

Lindsey glanced back at her and tried for a mocking laugh, unsuccessfully. "I promise you one thing — you're going to wish you'd never come back here."

"I've been wishing that ever since I arrived."

He turned away, took Mrs Hartman's arm and virtually pushed her out of the room; the action said, more plainly than any words, "You may have had power when you came into this room, but you sure as hell don't have any now."

Ryder nodded to Ruth. "I'll call you in the morning, Mrs Adams, when I've had a few ideas." Then he followed his ex-clients, leaving the three of us alone.

Marisa said, "That was *awful*, all of it."

Ruth sighed deeply and sat down. Her daughter and I did the same. Even I, the bystander, was exhausted — other people's emotion can be as wearing as one's own. I think we all expected Scott Hartman to reappear once the helicopter had racketed away, but Clemente, coming to collect the coffee cups (nobody had taken so much as a sip), said, "Mr Scott sleeps now. Bad day. Maybe sleeps long, I hope. You like drinks? Best gin sling? You like dinner?"

Ruth replied, "No, thank you, Clemente. We'd better go."

★ ★ ★

Nick had made up his mind only to report the servicing of the water heater; everything else was probably a product of his overactive imagination — he read too many thrillers. OK, so the day before he'd undergone an unsettling experience, but he wasn't a kid, he knew things like that happened all the time. The Lindsey character was undoubtedly a shithead but when he'd said, "Oh for Christ's sake, I haven't got time to waste on this punk," it was a perfectly normal reaction; Nick could hear his own father saying the same. And when Ruth and Marisa and I reappeared, shattered, he was sure he'd made the right decision; he told me about the service, and I waved the matter aside, a man with more important things on his mind. God help me!

We had stopped on the way home and had bought steaks and wine and everything else we could think of for a good meal well away from the outside world, of which we'd had quite enough for one day. I lit a fire — it isn't usually so cold in September — and after we'd eaten we sat around it, drinking wine and trying to sort out our impressions of the day by recounting them to Nick. He, though we couldn't know it, was more relieved than ever that he'd kept his suspicions to himself; they would have sounded petty and ridiculous compared with the dramas of Hawk Rock.

I don't think we even knew that we were really too tired to think constructively about what we proposed to do next day. Ruth was determined to see Scott Hartman again, this time by herself; alone with him, she could say things which could never be said in front of other people. I reminded her that if she wanted to go in the morning she'd have to take Marisa's car, mine would be absent for three or four hours while they serviced it; and in any case she'd better talk to Wesley Ryder before she again faced Hartman — he had said he'd call her.

In the meantime she was in two minds about telling Jack the whole story and asking him to bring their own attorney when he flew up on Saturday. She had no doubt that in the end Hartman could be dissuaded, and we agreed that Jack might be just the person to bring this about. He was used to dealing with difficult people, dealt with them by the dozen every working day, and his position as . . . not exactly the wronged husband, but certainly the good man who had saved the situation for Ruth, might catch Hartman off balance.

I don't suppose Ruth or Marisa or I would have been able to get to sleep for hours without first exhausting our already exhausted minds with plans and recapitulations. Nick just listened, putting the right questions at the

right moment and making the right
exclamations of amazement — bless
him. But how much more profitable
it would have been for all of us if
we hadn't talked so much and he had
talked more.

5

Cross-Eye

1

THE only thing to do with that Friday, a black Friday if ever there was one, is to describe it chronologically as each of us remembers it.

My alarm woke me at seven. I switched it off and was about to turn over and go back to sleep for a while when I remembered why I'd set it at that hour — the car. In spite of staying up late the night before, and in spite of all that talk, which should have exorcized the day, my turbulent brain had kept me awake until after two in the morning. I heaved myself off the sofa and sat on the edge of it, yawning and feeling sorry for myself. For the first time in five days I thought with regret of chapter nine and wondered when the Hartman debacle would sort itself out and allow me to get back to work, and back to my own bed which I missed.

After a couple of minutes I went to the bathroom, noting that all three bedroom doors were closed. One of the irritating things about having an apartment full of people is that every move has to be made as quietly as possible: so no shower — it made too much noise — and after shaving and washing, no fresh clothes — my closet was about a yard from Marisa's head. Ah well, I thought, there's always coffee. Glancing at the time, 7.25, I decided to have two cups before I went to the Ford dealers and get my breakfast when I returned, and my shower, family circumstances permitting.

By the time I left the house it was coming up to 7.45. Nobody else was stirring. The only likely candidate would have been Marisa who wakes early; Ruth lies in bed until around nine, and Nick would sleep through Armageddon if allowed to do so.

When I walked into the next-door vacant lot where we tenants keep our cars, I noticed that a van was parked on the street, blocking it — people often do this in spite of the two notices we've put up. I was relieved it hadn't been left there locked; a big young man was standing at the open door, arguing with a woman inside. As soon as he saw me he said, "OK, I'll move it." And then, before I'd reached the Taurus, "Pardon me, sir, you happen to know Lexington Avenue? We seem to have lost it."

I saw that the woman was staring at one of the useless street maps of Astoria which are all that can be obtained. I said, "Sure, I know Lexington — it's a long street; which part do you want?" I half leaned in at the open door, and the woman half held the map towards me. I was just reaching for it when I felt a sharp stinging sensation in my right thigh. I think I may have turned, may even have said, "Hey, what . . . ?" and then the big young man and the map and the woman swam out of focus and were gone.

★ ★ ★

Marisa had heard me leave the apartment and was lying awake thinking back over yesterday, that long, disordered, extraordinary day. She realized that it was useless, now, to wish she'd never made the journey to Oregon: as useless as wishing her mother and father had kept quiet about the circumstances of her birth. They hadn't and she'd come here, and look at the mess they were all in as a result! Scott Hartman and Christina Hartman and Mark Lindsey, all furiously angry, had haunted her dreams, lurching to and fro in huge, brilliantly lit rooms; even lying awake she found them larger than life, like the grotesque figures, twice man-size, she'd seen in a Mexican fiesta.

She heard Nick come out of the

junk room, go into the bathroom to relieve himself and stagger back to bed where, she knew, he'd snuggle down into virtually uninterrupted sleep for another hour, or even two. About ten minutes after he'd closed his door the phone rang. She glanced at her clock: 8.05. Knowing I was out and that the extension by her bed was the only one, she grabbed it quickly before it could disturb the others. A woman's voice, a pleasant, young voice, said, "Is this where Mr Adams — ?" And to someone nearby, "What? Oh. Sorry — is this where Mr Will Adams lives?"

"Yes."

"You his wife?"

"Niece."

"He was took kinda funny — in Safeway. I was right next to him."

"Funny — how do you mean?"

"Kinda passed out."

Marisa said, "Oh, how awful."

"He ain't bad, it's just . . . My husband was there too, we got him in our van."

Marisa wondered what I'd been doing in Safeway. Hadn't I gone to get my car serviced? The phone made rustling noises and a man, presumably the husband, said, "You want to come over and get him? I guess he didn't oughter drive, know what I mean?"

"Sure, I'll come right away. Where are you?"

"Parking lot . . . yeah, west side, near the American Legion. Know it?"

"Yes." She had sat outside the Legion for twenty minutes the day before yesterday while Nick and I were shopping.

"Don't seem no sense in calling Medix for five hundred bucks if you can pick him up."

"Right. I'll . . . I'll be there in about ten minutes. What color's your van?"

"Red. You'll see us — hardly anyone parked here anyway."

"Ten minutes." She pulled on jeans and T-shirt and loafers; thought of telling Nick and then thought better of it — he wasn't too bright when

310

woken suddenly.

It must have been about 8.25 when she reached the parking lot. The first thing she saw was my Taurus — odd, why wasn't it being serviced? — and not far away the red van. A big man was standing by the open door, peering inside. She jumped out of the station wagon and ran towards him. "Is he OK?"

"Nothing serious. This happen often?"

"I don't think so." She looked into the van and saw me propped up against the woman's ample bosom. "Oh God, he looks . . . " And that was as far as she got before she felt the jab in her thigh. She was aware of being propelled from behind, just aware of the woman reaching across me towards her . . .

★ ★ ★

Ruth awoke before Nick. She glanced at her watch: 9.05; then lay in bed for a few minutes, rehearsing the things

311

she wanted to say to Wesley Ryder, and then the much more personal things she intended to say to Scott Hartman when she got to Hawk Rock. She wasn't too good at talking tough but could manage it if necessary, and today it was necessary all right. Still occupied with her thoughts she got up, put on her robe, ran a comb through her hair and went to the bathroom; like most women, she doesn't shower or see to her face until after breakfast.

She had expected my sofa bed to be tidied away, but was surprised to notice that Marisa wasn't in her room; and wasn't in the kitchen either. She thought for a moment, and then went out to the hall and looked down into the street. The evening before, when we'd returned from Hawk Rock, Marisa's station wagon had been parked at the opposite curb; it wasn't there now. She went back to the kitchen and poured herself some coffee, thinking that her daughter must have woken early and gone with me to the Ford dealers in order to drive me back in her car. It struck her as odd that only a single coffee cup had apparently been used — one of us must have gone without. Also, if we'd both departed before eight o'clock, why weren't we back by now? She concluded that we must have gone to a restaurant for breakfast on our way home.

Presently, as she ate her toast, she heard Nick come out of the junk room. Three open doors told him that he was disturbing nobody, so he took his shower, singing as usual, and emerged twenty minutes later, shaved and shining. It was now 9.55. He was surprised to find Ruth on her own. She mentioned to him her guess that we were probably breakfasting out — Marisa's car wasn't in the street.

Immediately Nick's suspicions of the previous day came tumbling back into his mind; he'd been pretty sure they hadn't gone away but were waiting to pounce. He said, "But Will was due at Ford at eight; it wouldn't take them two hours to get breakfast."

Ruth hadn't been particularly worried until then, but his uneasiness communicated itself to her. She studied him for a second or two, then said, "You're a bit jumpy this morning. What's on your mind?"

"Nothing. I mean . . . I don't know really. OK, it was that guy who serviced the water heater."

"What about him?"

Nick told her what about him, omitting his more fanciful deductions. Ruth, being wise, understood exactly why he hadn't said any of this the night before: in the first place he'd have had a hard time getting a word in edgewise, and secondly, boys of that age are particularly sensitive about being thought unduly nervous or, as he put it himself, 'old womanish'. By the time he'd finished she was more or less convinced that there probably had been something doubtful about the man; and, as the minutes ticked by, there was certainly something doubtful about our continuing absence. Were they connected? She didn't believe in doubtful coincidences.

Nick said, "If they were going to be gone this long they'd have called, wouldn't they?"

Andy Swensen might almost have been standing outside my front door, waiting for his cue. The bell rang. Nick opened the door. Andy said, "Hi there! You folks had any phone calls this morning?"

"Not that I know of. Why?"

Andy peered past him, no doubt searching the apartment for signs of an orgy; he saw Ruth in her robe and gave her what he takes to be his winning smile. It wasn't returned, so he answered the question: "Mr Adams called. Tried to get you. Couldn't." He likes to milk any situation and now paused, forcing Ruth to ask, "Why couldn't he get us?"

"Phone musta been off the hook, I guess. So he calls my number. Handy Andy, that's me." One of the remarks indicating that he thinks he deserves a tip.

"Where was he?" asked Ruth, trying not to sound irritated. "What did he say?"

"Pretty girl's his niece, right?"

"Yes."

"Taken her out in his boat. 'Tell 'em,' he says, 'I've taken Marisa out in my boat.'"

Ruth and Nick exchanged a look, both astonished. Andy elaborated: "Not the kinda day I'd choose, but then this weather gets to me chest, know what I mean?"

Ruth said, "Thank you, Andy. Sorry you were troubled."

As Nick shut the door on him he was saying, "Forecast said clearing, but it don't look — "

They stood staring at one another. Ruth said, "In his boat? Without telling us?"

Nick made a face and went to inspect the phones; both were firmly on their rests. He lifted one to make sure and got the correct, dialing tone.

Ruth said, "Maybe they both woke early and . . . I don't know. If it was a beautiful morning it might make sense."

They looked at the grey overcast day outside the windows. "Only kind of. Marisa's not sold on the water, is she?"

"Putting it mildly."

"When Will took us out day before yesterday . . . Well, it was the day she met her dad, she wasn't feeling all that great."

"No, she wasn't."

"Sure didn't enjoy it much then."

Again they looked at each other in silence. Ruth said, "Better have yourself some breakfast, Nick."

He put bread in the toaster. "And what was all that about the phones?"

"They do sometimes go crazy."

He shrugged. "If it wasn't working, all the more reason they'd have come back — they wouldn't just walk out on us."

317

"And if we'd still been asleep they'd have left a note."

"Right." He stared at the toaster for a while, and suddenly raised his head, struck by a thought. "Yes," he said, put down his cup and left her alone.

He was back in less than a minute, stretched out a clenched hand towards her, and then opened it. Marisa's little soapstone toad sat on his palm regarding them. "On the table by her bed."

They both looked at the talisman, frowning; then he said, "The other day she had him in her hand the whole time we were on the water. One thing I know — like, I mean, *know* — she'd never go out in that boat 'less she took Cross-eye with her."

★ ★ ★

We were told, much later, that Marisa and I had been given jabs of something called Penthelamine. On an empty stomach it can knock you out in

318

less than fifteen seconds. It may act quickly but it certainly doesn't wear off quickly. All the same, my head was fairly clear; I knew at once where I was: lying on the floor of *Mary Celeste*'s tiny cabin. A hand was suspended above me, and I recognized it as Marisa's hand; evidently she was lying on the bunk.

My immediate thought was that if you wanted to hide a couple of unconscious people, the cabin of a shabby old boat moored at Greg Johansen's little marina wasn't a bad place to choose — out of season. After Labor Day Greg was seldom around: too busy hoisting craft from the water, using this or that local ramp; and, except for a few stoic fishermen, there wasn't a boat enthusiast to be seen, least of all on a dull day.

Lying there, moving my head to and fro in the hope of clearing it, I was faced with the unhelpful fact that this predicament was only an extension of everything which had gone before. There was a straight line ruled from the moment when Marisa had decided she must find her father to this moment in my old boat. But the fact was that even though we'd been warned — by Connie, by Scott Hartman's lethal selfishness, and by Mark Lindsey himself in no uncertain terms — circumstance had still bound us hand and foot: Marisa couldn't be halted until she'd met her father, and then her father couldn't be halted until he'd changed his will in her favor. It was the first time I'd been given such a close look at whatever it is that shapes our ends, rough hew them how we may, and I hoped it would be the last.

The odd thing is that I could still think of Lindsey as being a boorish fool. Hartman was going to guess what he'd done, and he'd be made to pay for it. You might say I hadn't yet appreciated the finer points of the situation.

Then something more practical percolated into my cloudy brain: the sound of water against *Mary Celeste*'s hull was not the sound of the Skipanon River gently slapping her at her berth, it was more lively than that; and to be sure she could roll a little when moored, but not as much as she was rolling right now; and I realized that a slight heaving motion was not just my head and stomach reacting to a knockout drug, it was the heaving of a swell — not much of a swell but unmistakable.

I rolled over and onto my knees — and had to stay like that for quite a while, on all fours, until some kind of balance asserted itself. Then, grasping the foot of the bunk and a sturdy coat hook above it, I managed to stand up. My watch swam in and out of focus but I could see that the time was 10.10, which meant I'd been unconscious for a good two hours. Marisa still was unconscious and I must say I wasn't sorry. Obviously she too had been given that lightning jab, but of course I wondered how they'd got hold of her in order to jab her.

I'd put on a pullover that dismal morning, but she was wearing only a T-shirt and jeans, and it was cold. I reached for a blanket and pulled it over her. She didn't stir. Then I turned to the matter in hand, specifically to *Mary Celeste*'s little radio. I didn't expect to find it in perfect working order, it never is, even at the best of times, but I also didn't expect to find that someone had beaten it to death with a hammer. I turned from its remains and looked at the cabin door; it was shut and, I was willing to bet, padlocked from the outside, the way I always leave it. Slightly claustrophobic by nature, I didn't like that idea at all.

But no, it wasn't locked. I don't know why this surprised me, because as soon as I wrenched it open (it's badly warped) I saw there'd been no need to lock us in. We were already out in the Columbia, just clearing the mouth of the Skipanon; the Columbia was our locked door — only a lunatic would have tried to escape by jumping into it.

I could see at a glance that there was no one else on *Mary Celeste* with us. Thank God, no confrontations — I couldn't have coped. And of course we weren't moving under our own power — I'd have heard the chug of the diesel as soon as I regained consciousness. That could only mean that we were drifting — someone had dumped us out here and let us drift. I don't think I was afraid, not as yet; but then I hadn't yet realized that this situation was every bit as terrifying as the two experiences by which I always judge terror: once, lying belly down in a cave tunnel, the rock pressing against my back, my companion had dropped our flashlight into a deep pool, leaving us in total darkness half a mile from the surface; once, the plane in which I was flying from Rome to Paris was hijacked by five young terrorists, all stoned. I thought to myself that if I'd survived those I could survive this.

I crawled up the three steps from the cabin to the diminutive cockpit. Yes, that was where we were, about a mile and a half from Greg Johansen's marina and moving at a steady speed due north across the Columbia towards Chinook on the Washington side; and if we were moving cross-stream at any speed at all, my sluggish brain informed me, we weren't drifting, we were being towed.

I pushed the cabin door shut, but it was a moment before I felt secure enough to stand up and look for'ard. The day was overcast, the sun showing infrequently as a silver disc. The wind was cold and strong, gusting even stronger, and owing to recent rain the river was in full spate. It wasn't a day I'd have chosen, or dared to choose, for voyaging on the Columbia — which might be the very reason we were being forced to do so.

Clinging to the top of the cabin I could see we were being towed by some kind of fishing boat, three men visible on board; the tow was unusually long, over a hundred feet. What with the overcast sky and a haze wind-whipped from the river, and I suppose the aftereffect of the drug, I couldn't see the boat at all clearly, and I don't think I'd have been able to place her anyway — there are several different types around. I guessed she was capable of more speed than we were now making, but I didn't want her to go any faster; I needed time to screw my head on properly and think. I ducked back into the cockpit where the cabin concealed me, wondering if the men had seen me and whether it mattered if they had. On the whole it seemed preferable that they should think I was still lying on the cabin floor. While I was huddled in the stern sheets we began to alter course, swinging westward towards Ilwaco and Cape Disappointment.

How comparatively simple it would be if I could start the diesel, crawl forward and cut the towline, then head for Hammond or the shore on either side of it. No, I still wasn't thinking straight. If they'd taken the trouble to disable the radio they would hardly have left the diesel in working order. When I finally managed to lift the engine hatch I found it untouched, but the battery had been removed and was no doubt sitting on the bottom of the Skipanon. So only the rudder was present and in one piece: not much use without an engine.

Around now it entered my head that if I hadn't worried so much about scaring the others, if I'd told them we were being watched, we might all have been more cautious. But would that have guaranteed safety? Probably not; we were clearly in the hands of experts who knew exactly what they were doing, and would hardly be disconcerted by any of the simple precautions we might take. I hoped Ruth and Nick were all right; I hoped they were aware of our disappearance.

The westward swing was continuing,

and we were passing Tansy Point, about a mile and a half from Hammond, two and a half from Buoy 12; and Buoy 12 marked the point beyond which I had long ago been warned never to take *Mary Celeste*. So — and it had to be faced — we were only five miles from the mouth of the Columbia, that graveyard of big ships; and on this foul day and at high tide the collision between river and ocean would be at its most deadly. If I was going to do anything, if there was in fact anything that could be done, I'd better get moving right now.

It was a frustrating and implacable situation, and quite unlike any I'd had to face before. Out there ahead of us were three uncaring and anonymous men who had no personal connection with us of any kind, nor ever would have; in their own time, at their own unhurried speed, they were trailing us along as if we were a load of industrial waste which they would ditch when they felt like it, letting the ocean scatter us and pulverize us, with *Mary Celeste II*, until the pieces were barely recognizable ('Writer and Niece in Columbia Tragedy') or never seen again ('Tragic Disappearance of . . . '). I didn't doubt that this was what was planned; I don't suppose I'd had any doubt from the moment I first opened my eyes, but nature imposes a kindly censorship so that we face things as and when we have the strength to do so. Hence my first drugged and ingenuous deduction that Mark Lindsey, or those that served him, didn't know what they were doing; they knew all right — boating accidents were rife all summer long.

So now I must pull myself together in no uncertain manner and take action. But what action? My head seemed to be empty of thought. I actually hit my forehead with a cold fist, like a child, as if this would get the brain moving. Perhaps it did. An idea, not a very brilliant one but at least an idea, came to me at the same moment as the cabin door grated open. Marisa stood there staring, blue eyes wide and frightened in a pale face. And, oh God, what was I going to tell her?

* * *

By 10.30 Ruth and Nick had made up their minds that the only thing they could sensibly do was get hold of a taxi, drive to the marina where I kept my boat, and see if we'd really gone sailing on such an unpromising day. Though Nick thought this out of the question, on account of the Cross-eye factor, he agreed that they couldn't begin to search elsewhere or even notify the police until they'd checked. He thanked God that I'd taken him to Greg Johansen's, or they wouldn't have had the slightest idea where to start looking — there are an awful lot of small boats clustered about the mouth of the Columbia.

Both he and Ruth were now sure in their own minds that something strange, perhaps disastrous, was going on. In the taxi Ruth said, "It always seems crazy when . . . when things like this come crashing into ordinary life." Nick kept quiet; he couldn't see anything in the least 'ordinary' about what we'd told him of our meetings with Scott Hartman, his wife, and Mark Lindsey whom he'd long ago accepted as being a dangerous thug; and he said nothing because he didn't want to add to her anxieties. In fact, Ruth was thinking the same thing. Lindsey had appeared out of nowhere, from the rough direction of Phoenix, and had managed to snare the prime heiress of the whole Pacific Northwest; how he'd managed to do this was not a mystery to her — she had appreciated from the first that he was sexy as well as vicious. It stood to reason that he'd be prepared to take almost any step, any risk, if he saw the whole solid-gold setup disappearing down the drain.

On that taxi ride she thought with misery of her refusal to tell Marisa her father's identity, and of the inner voice which had haunted her ever since she'd realized that their meeting couldn't be prevented. The truth of the matter seemed to be that they should never have revealed to Marisa that Jack wasn't her true father. Guilt writhed in her stomach and she felt sick. As much to herself as to the oddly reassuring boy beside her, she said, "Oh God, it's got to be all right, it's *got* to be."

By the time they reached Johansen's marina it was 10.55. The first thing they saw was Marisa's station wagon parked by the boat shed. Nick all but fell out of the taxi and began to run; it was the first time he had so obviously shown his fear. Ruth ran after him, stumbling over the rough ground. She found him on a wooden jetty staring at the empty berth. He wheeled around to face her. "Jesus! They did go."

The strange thing was that the absence of *Mary Celeste*, which in one way proved them wrong, had a much stronger opposite effect. He said, "OK, it sounds crazy, but she just *wouldn't* have gone without this." Ruth hadn't realized that he'd brought the soapstone toad with him. She knew just how crazy it sounded, but she also knew her daughter. Marisa had always relied on a strange assortment of talismans, and if someone has been like that all their sentient life they stay like that. No, the girl wouldn't have ventured out onto the water, which she feared, without Cross-eye. Not — and it was a stomach-churning thought — of her own volition. Weakly she said, "Then . . . where's the boat, Nick?"

He had a suspicion of what might have happened, though the mechanics of it defeated him; it was as wild (and as correct) as most of his other suspicions, but he wasn't going to dump it on Marisa's agonized mother. He looked about him wildly, but on that overcast weekday, with the season over, there were no helpful and perhaps informative yachtsmen around — there was nobody around. Marisa's car sat there looking at them, a vital but dumb witness. The north wind sent pieces of paper skittering along the side of the boat shed. A calico cat was stalking something among tufts of marshy grass.

Furiously Nick said, "Who the hell runs this place? There's never anyone here." Three minutes later, while they were looking for the office, an old pick-up rattled down the dusty lane and stopped beside the station wagon. Greg Johansen got out of it and said, "Hi! What can I do for you folks?"

When he saw the empty berth he shook his head: "Will never takes her out days like this."

It was lucky that Johansen was no periphery inhabitant of the waterfront; he had served his term in the navy and after that had shipped for seven years as a merchant seaman. Every real sailor knows all about superstition, and among the jumbled details of the story which Ruth and Nick now told him it was the Cross-eye factor, something most landsmen would have dismissed as being beside the point, that he found convincing and conclusive. He ran to his office, and by the time they'd caught up with him he was on the phone to someone called Brad; he was saying, "Hey, when you came in this morning, what were you telling Duane? Something about some small craft you saw."

"Sure. Out there by Buoy 10."

It seemed that as Brad was bringing his fishing boat back to the Skipanon he'd seen this little cabin cruiser following another fisherman towards the ocean. The wind, he said, was 'whupping up' the water and visibility wasn't too great, but he saw her all right; he and his son had thought it a bit silly, no weather for taking risks.

"Was she," demanded Johansen, "kind of funny-looking?"

"Yeah, sure was. Steered by tiller."

It didn't take Marisa long to grasp what was happening to us; lying on the bunk, trying to get mind and body in coordination, she'd already guessed some of it. When I'd filled in the gaps with what I hoped was a suitably censored, not-too-terrifying version of my own thoughts, she said, "But where are they taking us?"

I seized on this with relief: "Somewhere along the coast, I guess. Depends which way they turn when they reach the ocean. But there's a chance we can get away before then."

The more I thought of the idea the less feasible it seemed; but anything was worth trying, and any action was better than inaction. I took hold of the tiller and forced it slowly over to starboard; it was a basic contraption with no mechanism to assist it, and forcing it against the river's following current wasn't easy. After a second Marisa also grabbed it, helping me. "I don't see . . . "

But then she did see. Sure enough,

following current or not, the port rudder was slowly beginning to swing us inshore on the end of the tow. Beyond Hammond lie the open spaces preserved by Fort Stevens State Park, and there's a wide shallow bay between Point Adams and the last land of Clatsop Spit. Across it march the pilings which are all that remain of the railway, specially constructed for the mighty task of building the south jetty, a giant's causeway of immense boulders stretching more than two miles out into the Pacific. If we could continue to swing south on our puny little rudder it was just conceivable that we might run aground within wading distance of the shore; and once we were out of the fierce current and in the lee of the spit wading or swimming would present no problem; I could even see a couple of small boats there — I'm not sure what they fish for but they're usually around.

Now that we had turned sideways, propelled by three forces — the river, the towrope, the rudder — the Columbia's powerful current was actually helping us, catching us on the starboard beam, pushing us towards calm water and land. The idea was proving more effective than I could have believed; already the fishing boat lay clear on our right side, and we were heading in a different direction. With luck, and given this mediocre visibility, and if nobody on our escort looked back at us for another five minutes, we might just get away with it.

But then, I suppose inevitably, one of the men did look back and see what we were doing; there was a shout, and it ended our little bid for freedom. The fishing boat turned northwards across the channel, which happened at that moment to be quite free of other shipping, giving her all the room in the world to maneuver. Inexorably she began to haul us towards the Washington shore, and our swing in the opposite direction dwindled to nothing; we were being dragged back into that surging current, facing away from safety and directly into danger.

In a small sad voice Marisa said, "It nearly worked, didn't it?"

Nearly! I looked at her face, young and beautiful and touched now by a little color, and I felt a cold weight of dread in the pit of my stomach. How could I tell her what lay ahead? Or should I perhaps say nothing and simply let it happen? But wasn't it always better to know what was coming? Wasn't it infinitely more terrifying to be faced with disaster unwarned? I was aware of how intently she was watching my face, but I was quite unprepared to hear her say, "They're trying to kill us, aren't they?"

What a remarkable child she was, and what a strange age that is, particularly in women, who are so wise: poised between childhood and womanhood, slipping from one to the other without knowing it. I replied, "Yes. But they're not going to succeed."

"What's going to happen, Will?" And

because I returned her stare, almost angrily I think: "I can take it. I'd rather know."

The courage was so touching, and her youth so overwhelming, not to mention her grave beauty, that I found I couldn't speak; my throat was blocked. Oh great, Will Adams! All we need at a moment like this is a grown man in tears! Furiously I said, "We're going to get out of it. God knows how but we are."

The end of Clatsop Spit was creeping up on us now. I could see, across flat scrub and sand, the watchtower on the ocean side of it; I could see the jetty beyond, and gouts of spray where the Pacific breakers were pounding at it. Dead ahead, partially obscured by the top of *Mary Celeste*'s ugly little cabin, lay the terrible maelstrom of the bar where those breakers from one side and the plunging Columbia from the other could pulverize a small boat like this within a few minutes.

I said, "I think the idea is to make

it look like an accident. I think they mean to . . . tow us right onto the bar and . . . and slip the tow, and let the ocean do the rest."

I saw fear flit behind her eyes, and remembered her terror of water — and horses. Surprising me again, she said, "Don't look like that, Will. It isn't your fault — it's my fault. I shouldn't have come here."

I pulled her towards me and hugged her, and as I did so the little boat began to buck. Tremulously, into my shoulder, she said, "I don't have Cross-eye. If I'd brought Cross-eye . . . " She ended on a gasp. *Mary Celeste* had bucked again; green water rose over her bows and came slapping down on us. This was it. I turned and lurched down into the cabin; seized the life jacket and staggered back on deck, throwing it to her. "Put it on, quick."

"But you — "

"Marisa, quick."

By the time I'd jammed the cabin door shut and turned, she was struggling into it. I tied the straps, clumsily — my hands were freezing. *Mary Celeste* met another wave head on, and more icy water spattered across her. When she dipped into the next trough I expected to see that the towrope had been slipped, but it arose taut from the next plunging breaker. I realized they were going to hold us where we were. If they released us we might somehow, by some miracle, escape; but, held, mighty river and mighty ocean could keep slamming into us until we broke apart.

Marisa was clutching the gunwale, her face now a mask of terror; I'm sure mine was the same. The next wave hit us a juddering blow and we were suddenly ankle-deep in water — ankle-deep, and the gallant little boat was turning away from the onslaught as if she couldn't face any more of it, turning broadside on. I saw the wave coming, and at the same moment felt the river throwing us towards it. I reached out instinctively for Marisa just before we were deluged, went right under and, God knows how, rose out of it: in one piece but listing, listing towards the breaker which would follow and the one which would follow that if we hadn't capsized. It was, it really was, the maelstrom, each thrust of the river and each tumbling wave creating a whirlpool — water leaping over our heads in wind-whipped spray, and a terrible continuous roar, the endless anger of river and ocean at each other's throats.

The next wave came. *Mary Celeste* heeled right over. Marisa screamed. We were balancing over icy green depths. I leaned back, pulling her with me. We tipped the other way and nearly went overboard backwards. Then, blinded and gasping, I lost all sense of time or sequence. The roof of the cabin tore away, hung lopsided for an instant and was devoured. The next wave toppled onto the bunk, the broken radio, the little stove. The bows went down, a dead weight, and the stern rose up, exposing us to a surge of water which, God knows why, didn't sweep us away. The towrope had gone, the next wave was coming, towering; I suppose we were still in the boat but water was up to our waists. The noise was now deafening. I was looking up at the belly of a helicopter. The cabin door was torn off and sailed past our heads. I was still hanging on to Marisa. Another breaker fell on us, and something huge, dark and huge, was blotting out the sky; it had to be death . . .

But it wasn't death, it was a coastguard cutter which had wheeled around and now wallowed between us and that malevolent ocean. Ropes, nets, hands — and, oh God, Marisa had slipped away from me! For an agonizing moment I saw her in the water, under the water, and I was falling towards her. She was going to be crushed between the coastguard vessel and whatever was left of *Mary Celeste*: the river was going to crush her to death.

But then *Mary Celeste* reeled away from her and she was hauled up, gasping, choking, water streaming, but in one piece and not streaked with blood; and the river, as if tired of playing with us, swirled me towards the cutter's hull just as she heeled over towards me. I hit my head and went under yet again, but ropes held, hands held, and I was lying full-length beside Marisa on the deck, both of us spewing salt water.

Her eyes were closed and her pallor looked like the pallor of death. My heart missed a beat, several beats. I stretched out a hand and found her shoulder, gripped it, shook her hard. One blue eye opened — and closed again. She was all right. My head seemed to be bleeding freely.

People in extremity do strange things. Bleeding and dribbling and choking, I managed to raise myself a few inches, in spite of the fact that someone was trying to hold me down. I just had to see . . . There she was, but only just. The cabin had gone completely; the stumpy mast had gone. She was down by the bows, her little rudder waving to and fro as if in farewell. The next wave surged over her and she never reappeared. And I lay there and wept for that amazing, ugly little boat; she had kept us afloat just long enough for others to save us.

2

Marisa and I were both slightly drunk by the time we were reunited with Ruth and Nick — someone had given us brandy and sugar and hot water, a potent pick-me-up on empty stomachs. Marisa's mother and her best friend didn't mind at all — they were drunk themselves, with relief.

We owed our lives to the coastguards, no doubt about that, but also to Greg Johansen who knew all about emergencies at sea; he had been in a few himself. It hadn't mattered to him how or why *Mary Celeste* was out there beyond Buoy 9, heading for the mouth of the Columbia, the thing was to act first and ask questions later. The pilot of the coastguard helicopter had been astounded to see the towrope, but see it he did, and his colleague photographed it. A minute later it was slipped, but by then the people who mattered knew they weren't witnessing an accident, knew we'd been forced into that situation of extreme danger.

As soon as the cutter was in position between what was left of *Mary Celeste* and the savage ocean, he had racketed away northwards and had picked up the fishing boat before she even made Cape Disappointment. He ordered her to return to Astoria, but the skipper didn't obey, possibly hoping that the worsening visibility might protect him until he reached whatever refuge he had in mind; fishermen are nothing if not determined.

The three men have been charged with varying degrees of homicide, but so far no connection has been made between them and any third party, let alone a possible fourth or fifth party, all of whom would turn out to be go-betweens with no idea where their instructions originated. The state is sure that a little wheeling and dealing vis-à-vis the murder charge will eventually persuade one of the fishermen to break his silence, thus revealing the end of the chain. Two are in their twenties, the third in his teens. I wonder. And if one of them does talk, I wonder how much he'll really know.

When it came to Marisa and I giving the law our version of events, it was difficult to decide what to say, and even more difficult to decide what to leave out. My brother Jack, at his best in this kind of situation, perceived that the only possible course was for us to dump our whole mess of evidence on the rich man's table. Let Scott Hartman be the one to determine how much or how little he wanted the authorities to know about his family and his private affairs, not to mention his own less than admirable part in the proceedings. My guess is that nobody will ever know very much.

The police are well aware of the fact that the whole thing hangs on the individual who came to 'service' the water heater — briefed, needless to say, by those watchers who had monitored all our movements. Nick had obviously been correct about the man's tools; he had spent two hours excavating my life, picking the locks on my desk, etcetera. Among other artifacts, he unearthed *Mary Celeste*'s papers and receipts for the monthly mooring fee I paid to Greg Johansen. I imagine some faceless superior decided that when it came to accidental death, this was the best of several options at their disposal. Obviously it's difficult to say what the other options were, since only the one which was put into practice can be investigated — partially. A first alternative seems to have featured accident or perhaps suicide, making use of my gun which had been locked in the bottom drawer of the desk but was found to be missing. A second involved Marisa's station wagon; apparently this device would have wrecked the vehicle once a certain speed was reached. The police are very cagey about it — it's a new trick, and not one they want other people to copy.

Of course my diary, with its information that the car was due for a service at eight o'clock, certainly influenced the choice; moreover the Taurus was conveniently parked with three others in the vacant lot next door, where laurels and trees screened it on either side and where the red van would stop my abduction being seen from the house across the street. They also wove their plan around the fact that the apartment only had a single extension phone, in my bedroom, at that time being used by Marisa; her few cosmetics and her clothing would have made it clear who was sleeping there. Early in the morning — or at least early after a busy preceding day and a late going to bed, both of which had been observed — it was more than likely that she would answer any call — as she did. If this had failed, if any of their calculations had failed, I'm sure alternative arrangements had been made to separate her from her mother and Nick; and I could have been kept on ice until one of them was successful. As for Andy Swensen, I shall always wonder whether the heating engineer or some unknown person assessed him so precisely: a perfect fool who, on the phone, wouldn't know my voice from Donald Duck's.

The only component which no one can explain is the pick-up with mountain wheels which forced Marisa and Nick off the freeway. Was the driver a dangerous drunk trying to scare and impress a pretty girl, or was he really an ill-considered extension of Mark Lindsey's equally dangerous ego?

Police and State are sure that time will answer these and many other questions. I don't agree; I have a steadfast, if regretful, belief in the superior power of big money. The Hartmans have had a finger in every Northwestern pie for four or five generations. Their influence may not be as overwhelming as it once was, but it stands out a mile that anonymous operators must have been deployed to bring various Hartman conscripts into play against us — very efficiently and very quickly. The speed alone proves that a network already existed and had probably been operating outside the law for many years — with or without the law's connivance. The Sicilian gentlemen may run the biggest family organization but it isn't the only one in the United States, not by a long chalk.

I have no wish to denigrate Scott Hartman whom I've grown to admire. He was incoherent with rage when he first heard what had happened — rage and guilt, because he understood (at last, at long last) that his determination to change his will, his refusal to treat any of us as more than pawns on his private board, had nearly been responsible for the death of his own daughter.

Hawk Rock was soon buzzing with attorneys and high-ranking policemen and even a politician or two. That was part of the public face; but let's not forget that he's a Hartman, he's *the* Hartman. He has nothing to gain if the case is 'solved', so I imagine he's been making quite sure that it isn't solved. Private retribution within the family is another matter. I first got wind of this from Connie Sherwood King who called me about two weeks after our near-drowning. Naturally she didn't mention anything so unmannerly as cause and effect, but as usual she knows, if not everything, a great deal more than any other mere observer — and much more than the media which is still having a field day in total ignorance; but they must be used to that.

She said, "Seems you couldn't stop

your pretty girl going over the precipice."

I replied, "Connie, when did you last try stopping a youngster from doing what it wants?"

"Anyway I'm glad you survived the fall — *both* of you. I wondered if you'd heard today's news, hot from wherever today's news is minted?"

"In Astoria! Of course not."

"Susan Hartman is divorcing the revolting Lindsey."

When I'd found my breath I said, "My God, she might as well have shot him between the eyes."

"Would have been kinder, wouldn't it?"

On her last visit to Hawk Rock, Ruth had actually seen Susan, evidently summoned by her father. I think this is where retribution, rather than justice, comes in. Obviously he told her a few of the things her husband had done, and I daresay Marisa and I were quite minor details. Hence the divorce, hence the end of Mark Lindsey who will disappear and probably take to drink.

The fact that no crime will be pinned on him in public and legally is beside the point. Nor does it matter how well he may have lined his pocket with Hartman money; it won't satisfy him. The great golden ship will have sunk with all hands, taking his self-assurance with her. You don't get second chances like that.

I imagine a macabre silence has descended on Number Seven, EastWest Drive, as if it had been put to sleep, cobweb-covered, weed-entwined, awaiting the kiss which will bring it back to life; but it may be a long time before any prince dismounts under that porte-cochere. Does Christina Hartman wander in and out of the huge rooms, wondering why people no longer call, unaware as yet that the life she so ruthlessly contrived for herself is over? How much did she know of what her son-in-law proposed to do? I'm sure there were no overt discussions, merely an occasional meeting of cold eyes, and always that meeting of like minds: an unspoken agreement that he could do as he wished as long as she knew nothing — that would be her style. I wonder what will happen to her. Connie may one day tell me.

As for Scott Hartman himself, I suppose he'll continue to divide his days between those blinding windows and the well-thumbed books in his library. As I've said before, it seems a great waste of the enormous fortune, but if that's what he wants, if that's all his wasted body can bear . . .

In view of what happened at the mouth of the Columbia, it wasn't difficult for Jack to subvert Hartman's intentions regarding Marisa, but apparently he has insisted on setting up a trust for her. I'm sure she'll make good use of it . . . which leads us to the mere mortals.

Ruth and Jack returned to LA as soon as possible, primarily to thrust Marisa and Nick into their respective schools where they're both having to work hard to get the grades expected of them. I'm happy to report that Marisa's discovery of her real father, which might have had disastrous emotional consequences, was nullified by the things which arose from it. Since we were rescued in the nick of time I suppose we can now say that some good came out of our alarming ordeal by water. Perhaps I was correct in my first estimation, made in ignorance when she first appeared at the apartment: that knowing who her father was didn't matter much in the end and could be dismissed, whereas not knowing mattered like hell and could never be dismissed. Well, she knows, and the result, thank God, is that she and Jack are now closer than they've ever been.

I need hardly add that our shared experience of terror has forged an iron link between my niece and myself, one which may never be broken. I'm sure she sometimes wakes up shocked and sweating, as I do, with cold green water closing over her head. Ruth writes that Cross-eye is now somewhat out of favor and seems to have been replaced by a hideous jade ring, also a gift from her best friend. Ruth guesses that Marisa's reason for liking the ring is that she can keep an eye on it, and can touch it merely by crossing her fingers; this insures it will never get left behind if she takes any more trips on water. I look at the matter from a different point of view: because if Cross-eye hadn't been left behind, waiting for Nick to remember and discover him, Marisa wouldn't be around to wear the hideous ring and I wouldn't be around to tell the tale.

The pair of them propose to revisit me when their studies allow. I look forward to seeing them again. I think of them a lot, and I sincerely hope that they — intelligent, loyal, courageous — are the teenage future of America, rather than those others we all know too well.

The Columbia is preparing itself for winter. Greg Johansen's Indian summer never arrived. Since I no longer have

Mary Celeste to go pottering with I really didn't miss it, but I certainly miss my old boat; in fact, I miss her so much that when Scott Hartman thoughtfully offered to buy me a new, fast and seaworthy replacement I didn't accept. Stupid? Pig-headed? Probably. One day I may replace her myself, with something equally old and eccentric.

This morning I opened the file at chapter nine and read, 'Lewis returned to the mouth of the Columbia in November 1927 . . . ' The handwriting looked as if it belonged to someone else — I always write by hand, using the word processor for a fair copy.

After I'd gazed at chapter nine for a while with a blank mind I realized the cause of this unexpected block. I pulled some fresh pages towards me and wrote, 'I heard the other day about a man who was having breakfast, reading the paper and minding his own business, when a bulldozer came crashing through the wall of his house . . . '

A FOOT IN THE GRAVE
Bruce Marshall

About to be imprisoned and tortured in Buenos Aires, John Smith escapes, only to become involved in an aeroplane hijacking.

DEAD TROUBLE
Martin Carroll

Trespassing brought Jennifer Denning more than she bargained for. She was totally unprepared for the violence which was to lie in her path.

HOURS TO KILL
Ursula Curtiss

Margaret went to New Mexico to look after her sick sister's rented house and felt a sharp edge of fear when the absent landlady arrived.